Anonymous

Select Poems

Anonymous

Select Poems

ISBN/EAN: 9783744763974

Printed in Europe, USA, Canada, Australia, Japan

Cover: Foto ©Andreas Hilbeck / pixelio.de

More available books at **www.hansebooks.com**

SELECT.

POEMS.

PRINTED IN

1795.

ELEGY,

WRITTEN IN A COUNTRY CHURCH-YARD.

BY MR. GRAY.

T H E curfew tolls the knell of parting day,
The lowing herd wind flowly o'er the lea,
The ploughman homeward plods his weary way,
And leaves the world to darknefs and to me.

Now fades the glimmering landfcape on the fight,
And all the air a folemn ftillnefs holds,
Save where the beetle wheels his droning flight,
And drowfy tinklings lull the diftant folds;

Save that, from yonder ivy-mantled tow'r,
The moping owl does to the moon complain
Of fuch, as wand'ring near her fecret bow'r
Moleft her ancient folitary reign.

Beneath thofe rugged elms, that yew-tree's fhade,

Where heaves the turf in many a mould'ring heap,

Each in his narrow cell for ever laid,

The rude forefathers of the hamlet fleep.

The breezy call of incenfe-breathing Morn,

The fwallow twitt'ring from the ftraw-built fhed,

The cock's fhrill clarion, or the echoing horn,

No more fhall roufe them from their lowly bed:

For them no more the blazing hearth fhall burn,

Or bufy houfewife ply her evening care:

No children run to lifp their fire's return,

Or climb his knees the envied kifs to fhare.

Oft did the harveft to their fickle yield,

Their furrow oft the ftubborn glebe has broke:

How jocund did they drive their team afield!

How bow'd the woods beneath their fturdy ftroke!

Let

Let not Ambition mock their ufeful toil,

Their homely joys, and deftiny obfcure;

Nor Grandeur hear, with a difdainful fmile,

The fhort and fimple annals of the poor.

The boaft of heraldry, the pomp of pow'r,

And all that beauty, all that wealth e'er gave,

Await alike th' inevitable hour;

The paths of glory lead but to the grave.

Nor you, ye proud, impute to thefe the fault,

If Mem'ry o'er their tomb no trophies raife,

Where thro' the long-drawn ifle, and fretted vault,

The pealing anthem fwells the note of praife.

Can ftoried urn, or animated buft,

Back to its manfion call the fleeting breath?

Can Honour's voice provoke the filent duft,

Or Flatt'ry footh the dull cold ear of Death?

Perhaps

Perhaps in this neglected fpot is laid
Some heart once pregnant with celeftial fire;
Hands, that the rod of empire might have fway'd,
Or wak'd to ecftacy the living lyre:

But Knowledge to their eyes her ample page,
Rich with the fpoils of Time, did ne'er unroll;
Chill Penury reprefs'd their noble rage,
And froze the genial current of the foul.

Full many a gem of pureft ray ferene
The dark unfathom'd caves of Ocean bear:
Full many a flower is born to blufh unfeen,
And wafte its fweetnefs on the defert air.

Some village Hampden, that with dauntlefs breaft
The little Tyrant of his fields withftood;
Some mute inglorious Milton here may reft,
Some Cromwell guiltlefs of his country's blood.

Th'

Th' applause of lift'ning senates to command,

The threats of pain and ruin to despise,

To scatter plenty o'er a smiling land,

And read their history in a nation's eyes,

Their lot forbad: nor circumscrib'd alone

Their growing virtues, but their crimes confin'd;

Forbad to wade through slaughter to a throne,

And shut the gates of mercy on mankind;

The struggling pangs of conscious Truth to hide,

To quench the blushes of ingenuous Shame,

Or heap the shrine of Luxury and Pride

With incense kindled at the Muse's flame.

Far from the madding crowd's ignoble strife,

Their sober wishes never learn'd to stray;

Along the cool sequester'd vale of life

They kept the noiseless tenor of their way.

Yet

Yet ev'n thefe bones from infult to protect,
Some frail memorial ftill erected nigh,
With uncouth rhymes and fhapelefs fculpture deck'd,
Implores the paffing tribute of a figh:

Their name, their years, fpelt by th' unletter'd Mufe,
The place of fame and elegy fupply;
And many a holy text around fhe ftrews,
That teach the ruftic moralift to die.

For who, to dumb Forgetfulnefs a prey,
This pleafing anxious being e'er refign'd,
Left the warm precincts of the cheerful day,
Nor caft one longing ling'ring look behind!

On fome fond breaft the parting foul relies,
Some pious drops the clofing eye requires;
Ev'n from the tomb the voice of Nature cries,
Awake and faithful to her wonted fires.

For

For thee, who mindful of th' unhonour'd Dead
Doſt in theſe lines their artleſs tale relate;
If chance, by lonely Contemplation led,
Some kindred Spirit ſhall inquire thy fate,

Haply ſome hoary-headed ſwain may ſay,
' Oft have we ſeen him at the peep of dawn,
' Bruſhing with haſty ſteps the dews away
' To meet the ſun upon the upland lawn:

' There at the foot of yonder nodding beech,
' That wreathes its old fantaſtic roots ſo high,
' His liſtleſs length at noontide would he ſtretch,
' And pore upon the brook that babbles by.

' Hard by yon wood, now ſmiling, as in ſcorn,
' Mutt'ring his wayward fancies he would rove,
' Now drooping, woeful wan, like one forlorn,
' Or craz'd with care, or croſs'd in hopeleſs love.

　　　　　' One

' One morn I mifs'd him on the cuftom'd hill,

' Along the heath, and near his favourite tree;

' Another came; nor yet befide the rill,

' Nor up the lawn, nor at the wood was he:

' The next, with dirges due in fad array,

' Slow through the church-way path we faw him borne:

' Approach and read (for thou canft read) the lay,

' Grav'd on the ftone, beneath yon aged thorn.

' There fcatter'd oft, the earlieft of the year,

' By hands unfeen are fhow'rs of violets found;

' The redbreaft loves to build and warble there,

' And little footfteps lightly print the ground.'

THE

Here rests his head upon the lap of Earth
A Youth, to Fortune and to Fame unknown:
Fair Science frown'd not on his humble birth,
And Melancholy mark'd him for her own.

Large was his bounty, and his soul sincere,
Heav'n did a recompence as largely send:
He gave to Mis'ry all he had, a tear,
He gain'd from Heav'n ('twas all he wish'd) a friend.

No farther seek his merits to disclose,
Or draw his frailties from their dread abode,
(There they alike in trembling hope repose)
The bosom of his Father and his God.

ODE

ODE

ON A YOUNG LADY ATTENDING HER MOTHER.

BY MISS AIKIN.

W H E N blooming beauty, in the noon of power,

While offer'd joys demand each fprightly hour,

With all that pomp of charms and winning mien,

Which, fure to conquer, needs but to be feen;

When fhe, whofe name the fofteft love infpires,

To the hufh'd chamber of difeafe retires,

To watch and weep befide a parent's bed,

Catch the faint voice, and raife the languid head,

What mixt delight each feeling heart muft warm!

An angel's office fuits an angel's form!

Thus the tall column graceful rears its head

To prop fome mould'ring tow'r with mofs o'erfpread,

Whofe ftately piles and arches yet difplay

The venerable graces of decay:

Thus

Thus round the wither'd trunk fresh shoots are seen

To shade their parent with a cheerful green.

More health, dear Maid! thy soothing presence brings,

Than purest skies, or salutary springs.

That voice, those looks, such healing virtues bear,

Thy sweet reviving smiles might cheer despair;

On the pale lips detain the parting breath,

And bid hope blossom in the shades of death.

Beauty, like thine, could never reach a charm

So pow'rful to subdue, so sure to warm.

On her lov'd child behold the mother gaze,

In weakness pleas'd, and smiling thro' decays,

And leaning on that breast her cares assuage;—

How soft a pillow for declining age!

For this, when that fair frame must feel decay,

(Ye fates protract it to a distant day!)

When thy approach no tumults shall impart,

Nor that commanding glance strike thro' the heart;

When

When meaner beauties ſhall have leave to ſhine,

And crowds divide the homage lately thine;

Not with the tranſient praiſe thoſe charms can boaſt

Shall thy fair fame and gentle deeds be loſt:

Some pious hand ſhall thy weak limbs ſuſtain,

And pay thee back theſe generous cares again;

Thy name ſhall flouriſh, by the good approv'd, .

Thy memory honour'd, and thy duſt belov'd.

ODE

ODE
TO WISDOM.
BY THE SAME.

O wisdom! if thy soft controul
Can sooth the sickness of the soul,
Can bid the warring passions ceafe,
And breathe the calm of tender peace;
Wisdom! I bless thy gentle sway,
And ever, ever will obey.

But if thou com'st with frown auftere
To nurfe the brood of care and fear,
To bid our sweeteft passions die,
And leave us in their room a sigh;
Or, if thine afpect stern have power
To wither each poor tranfient flower
That cheers the pilgrimage of woe,
And dry the springs whence hope should flow;

Wisdom,

Wifdom, thine empire I difclaim,

Thou empty boaft of pompous name!

In gloomy fhades of cloifters dwell,

But never haunt my cheerful cell.

Hail to pleafure's frolic train!

Hail to fancy's golden reign!

Feftive mirth, and laughter wild,

Free and fportful as the child!

Hope, with eager fparkling eyes,

And eafy faith, and fond furprize!

Let thefe, in fairy colours dreft,

For ever fhare my carelefs breaft:

Then, tho' wife I may not be,

The wife themfelves fhall envy me.

ODE

ODE

ON THE DEATH OF COL. ROSS.

BY MR. W. COLLINS.

I.

WHILE, loſt to all his former mirth,
Britannia's genius bends to earth,
　And mourns the fatal day;
While, ſtain'd with blood, he ſtrives to tear
Unſeemly from his ſea-green hair
　The wreaths of cheerful May;

II.

The thoughts which muſing pity pays,
And fond remembrance loves to raiſe,
　Your faithful hours attend;
Still fancy, to herſelf unkind,
Awakes to grief the ſoften'd mind,
　And points the bleeding friend.

III. By

III.

By rapid Scheld's defcending wave
His country's vows fhall blefs the grave,

Where-e'er the youth is laid:
That facred fpot the village hind
With ev'ry fweeteft turf fhall bind,

And peace protect the fhade.

IV.

O'er him, whofe doom thy virtues grieve,
Aërial forms fhall fit at eve,

And bend the penfive head!
And, fall'n to fave his injur'd land,
Imperial Honour's awful hand

Shall point his lonely bed!

V.

The warlike dead of every age,
Who fill the fair recording page,

Shall leave their fainted reft:
And, half-reclining on his fpear,
Each wondering Chief by turns appear,

To hail the blooming gueft.

VI. Old

VI.

Old EDWARD's fons, unknown to yield,
Shall crowd from CRESSY's laurell'd field,
 And gaze with fix'd delight;
Again for Britain's wrongs they feel,
Again they fnatch the gleamy fteel,
 And wifh th' avenging fight.

VII.

If, weak to footh fo foft an heart,
Thefe pictur'd glories nought impart
 To dry thy conftant tear;
If yet in forrow's diftant eye,
Expos'd and pale thou feeft him lie,
 Wild war infulting near;

VIII.

Where-e'er from time thou court'ft relief,
The Mufe fhall ftill with focial grief
 Her gentle promife keep:
Ev'n humble HARTING's cottag'd vale
Shall learn the fad repeated tale,
 And bid her fhepherds weep.

C   O D E,

ODE,

WRITTEN IN THE YEAR 1745.

BY THE SAME.

How ſleep the brave, who ſink to reſt,
By all their country's wiſhes bleſt!
When Spring, with dewy fingers cold,
Returns to deck their hallow'd mould,
She there ſhall dreſs a ſweeter ſod
Than Fancy's feet have ever trod.

By fairy hands their knell is rung,
By forms unſeen their dirge is ſung:
There Honour comes, a Pilgrim grey,
To bleſs the turf that wraps their clay,
And Freedom ſhall awhile repair,
To dwell a weeping Hermit there!

THE GARLAND.

BY M. PRIOR.

I.

The pride of every grove I chofe,
  The violet fweet, and lily fair,
The dappled pink, and blufhing rofe,
  To deck my charming Chloe's hair.

II.

At morn the Nymph vouchfaf'd to place
  Upon her brow the various wreath;
The flowers lefs blooming than her face,
  The fcent lefs fragrant than her breath.

III.

The flowers fhe wore along the day:
  And every nymph and fhepherd faid,
That in her hair they look'd more gay
  Than glowing in their native bed.

C 2   IV. Undreft

IV.

Undreſt at evening, when ſhe found
  Their odours loſt, their colours paſt,
She chang'd her look, and on the ground
  Her garland and her eyes ſhe caſt.

V.

That eye dropt ſenſe diſtinct and clear,
  As any Muſe's tongue could ſpeak;
When from its lid a pearly tear
  Ran trickling down her beauteous cheek.

VI.

Diſſembling what I knew too well,
  My love, my life, ſaid I, explain
This change of humour: pr'ythee tell;
  That falling tear—what does it mean?

VII.

She ſigh'd; ſhe ſmil'd; and to the flowers
  Pointing, the lovely moraliſt ſaid:
See, friend, in ſome few fleeting hours,
  See yonder what a change is made;

VIII. Ah

VIII.

Ah me! the blooming pride of May
And that of beauty are but one :
At morn both flourifh bright and gay,
 Both fade at evening, pale and gone.

IX.

At dawn poor STELLA danc'd and fung;
 The amorous youth around her bow'd;
At night her fatal knell was rung;
 I faw, and kifs'd her in her fhrowd!

X.

Such as fhe is who died to-day,
 Such I, alas! may be to-morrow :
Go, DAMON, bid thy Mufe difplay
 The juftice of thy CHLOE's forrow.

HYMN.

H Y M N.

BY MR. ADDISON.

I.

THE ſpacious firmament on high,
With all the blue ethereal ſky,
And ſpangled heavens, a ſhining frame,
Their great original proclaim:
Th' unwearied ſun, from day to day,
Doth his Creator's power diſplay,
And publiſhes to every land
The work of an Almighty hand.

II.

Soon as the evening ſhades prevail,
The moon takes up the wondrous tale,
And nightly to the liſtening earth
Repeats the ſtory of her birth:
Whilſt all the ſtars that round her burn,
And all the planets in their turn,

Confirm

Confirm the tidings as they roll,

And ſpread the truth from pole to pole.

III.

What though, in ſolemn ſilence, all

Move round this dark terreſtrial ball!

What though nor real voice nor ſound

Amidſt their radiant orbs be found!

In reaſon's ear they all rejoice,

And utter forth a glorious voice,

For ever ſinging, as they ſhine,

" The hand that made us is Divine."

HYMN.

H Y M N.

I.

W H E N all thy mercies, O my God,

    My rifing foul furveys;

Tranfported with the view, I'm loft

    In wonder, love, and praife:

II.

O how fhall words with equal warmth

    The gratitude declare,

That glows within my ravifh'd heart?

    But thou canft read it there.

III.

Thy providence my life fuftain'd,

    And all my wants redreft,

When in the filent womb I lay,

    And hung upon the breaft.

IV. To

IV.

To all my weak complaints and cries
   Thy mercy lent an ear,
Ere yet my feeble thoughts had learnt
   To form themfelves in prayer.

V.

Unnumber'd comforts to my foul
   Thy tender care beftow'd,
Before my infant heart conceiv'd
   From whom thofe comforts flow'd.

VI.

When in the flippery paths of youth
   With heedlefs fteps I ran,
Thine arm unfeen convey'd me fafe,
   And led me up to man:

VII.

Through hidden dangers, toils, and deaths,
   It gently clear'd my way,
And through the pleafing fnares of vice,
   More to be fear'd than they.

VIII. When

VIII.

When worn with ficknefs, oft haft thou
  With health renew'd my face;
And, when in fins and forrows funk,
  Reviv'd my foul with grace.

IX.

Thy bounteous hand with worldly blifs
  Has made my cup run o'er,
And in a kind and faithful friend
  Haft doubled all my ftore.

X.

Ten thoufand, thoufand precious gifts
  My daily thanks employ,
Nor is the leaft a chearful heart,
  That taftes thofe gifts with joy.

XI.

Through every period of my life
  Thy goodnefs I'll purfue;
And after death in diftant worlds
  The glorious theme renew.

XII. When

XII.

When nature fails, and day and night
  Divide thy works no more,
My ever-grateful heart, O Lord,
  Thy mercy fhall adore.

XIII.

Through all eternity to thee
  A joyful fong I'll raife,
For, Oh! eternity's too fhort
  To utter all thy praife.

HYMN.

H Y M N.

BY THE SAME.

I.

WHEN rifing from the bed of death,
 O'erwhelm'd with guilt and fear,
I fee my Maker, face to face,
 Oh how fhall I appear!

II.

If yet while pardon may be found,
 And mercy may be fought,
My heart with inward horror fhrinks,
 And trembles at the thought;

III.

When thou, O Lord, fhalt ftand difclos'd
 In majefty fevere,
And fit in judgment on my foul,
 Oh how fhall I appear!

IV. But

IV.

But thou haſt told the troubled mind,

Who does her ſins lament,

The timely tribute of her tears

Shall endleſs woe prevent.

V.

Then ſee the ſorrow of my heart,

Ere yet it be too late ;

And hear my Saviour's dying groans,

To give thoſe ſorrows weight.

VI.

For never ſhall my ſoul deſpair

Her pardon to procure,

Who knows thy only Son has died

To make that pardon ſure.

ON

ON THE DEATH OF ADDISON.

BY MR. TICKEL.

If, dumb too long, the drooping Mufe hath ftay'd,
And left her debt to ADDISON unpaid;
Blame not her filence, WARWICK, but bemoan,
And judge, oh judge, my bofom by your own.
What mourner ever felt poetic fires?
Slow comes the verfe, that real woe infpires:
Grief unaffected fuits but ill with art,
Or flowing numbers with a bleeding heart.

   Can I forget the difmal night, that gave
My foul's beft part for ever to the grave!
How filent did his old companions tread,
By midnight lamps, the manfions of the dead;
Thro' breathing ftatues, then unheeded things,
Thro' rows of warriors, and thro' walks of kings!
What awe did the flow folemn knell infpire;
The pealing organ, and the paufing choir;

The

The duties by the lawn-rob'd prelate pay'd;

And the laſt words, that duſt to duſt convey'd!

While ſpeechleſs o'er thy cloſing grave we bend,

Accept theſe tears, thou dear departed friend,

Oh! gone for ever, take this long adieu;

And ſleep in peace, next thy lov'd MONTAGU!

 To ſtrew freſh laurels let the taſk be mine,

A frequent pilgrim at thy ſacred ſhrine;

Mine with true ſighs thy abſence to bemoan,

And grave with faithful epitaph thy ſtone.

If e'er from me thy lov'd memorial part,

May ſhame afflict this alienated heart;

Of thee forgetful if I form a ſong,

My lyre be broken, and untun'd my tongue;

My grief be doubled, from thy image free,

And mirth a torment, unchaſtis'd by thee.

 Oft let me range the gloomy iſles alone,

(Sad luxury! to vulgar minds unknown)

Along the walls where ſpeaking marbles ſhow

What worthies form the hallow'd mould below:

Proud

Proud names, who once the reins of empire held;

In arms who triumph'd; or in arts excell'd;

Chiefs, grac'd with scars, and prodigal of blood;

Stern patriots, who for sacred freedom stood;

Just men, by whom impartial laws were given;

And saints, who taught, and led the way to heaven.

Ne'er to these chambers, where the mighty rest,

Since their foundation, came a nobler guest;

Nor e'er was to the bowers of bliss convey'd

A fairer spirit, or more welcome shade.

In what new region, to the just assign'd,

What new employments please th' unbody'd mind?

A winged virtue, through th' ethereal sky,

From world to world unwearied does he fly?

Or curious trace the long laborious maze

Of Heaven's decrees, where wondering Angels gaze?

Does he delight to hear bold Seraphs tell

How Michael battled, and the Dragon fell?

Or, mix'd with milder Cherubim, to glow

In hymns of love, not ill essay'd below?

Or

Or doſt thou warn poor mortals left behind?

A taſk well ſuited to thy gentle mind!

Oh! if ſometimes thy ſpotleſs form deſcend,

To me thy aid, thou guardian genius, lend!

When age miſguides me, or when fear alarms,

When pain diſtreſſes, or when pleaſure charms,

In ſilent whiſperings purer thoughts impart,

And turn from ill a frail and feeble heart;

Lead through the paths thy virtue trod before,

'Till bliſs ſhall join, nor death can part us more.

That aweful form (which, ſo the heavens decree,

Muſt ſtill be lov'd, and ſtill deplor'd by me)

In nightly viſions ſeldom fails to riſe,

Or, rous'd by fancy, meet my waking eyes:

If buſineſs calls, or crowded courts invite,

Th' unblemiſh'd ſtateſman ſeems to ſtrike my ſight;

If in the ſtage I ſeek to ſooth my care,

I meet his ſoul, which breathes in CATO there;

If penſive to the rural ſhades I rove,

His ſhape o'ertakes me in the lonely grove:

D   'Twas

'Twas there of juft and good he reafon'd ftrong,

Clear'd fome great truth, or rais'd fome ferious fong;

There patient fhow'd us the wife courfe to fteer,

A candid cenfor, and a friend fincere;

There taught us how to live; and (oh! too high

The price for knowledge!) taught us how to die.

Thou hill, whofe brow the antique ftructures grace,

Rear'd by bold chiefs of WARWICK's noble race,

Why, once fo lov'd, whene'er thy bower appears,

O'er my dim eye-balls glance the fudden tears!

How fweet were once thy profpects frefh and fair,

Thy floping walks and unpolluted air!

How fweet the gloom beneath thy aged trees,

Thy noon-tide fhadow, and thy evening breeze!

His image thy forfaken bowers reftore;

Thy walks and airy profpects charm no more;

No more the fummer's in thy gloom allay'd,

Thy evening breezes, and thy noon-day fhade.

From other ills, however fortune frown'd,

Some refuge in the Mufe's art I found;

Reluctant

Reluctant now I touch the trembling ſtring,

Bereft of him, who taught me how to ſing ;

And theſe ſad accents, murmur'd o'er his urn,

Betray that abſence, they attempt to mourn.

Oh! muſt I then (now freſh my boſom bleeds,

And CRAGGS in death to ADDISON ſucceeds)

The verſe, begun to one loſt friend, prolong,

And weep a ſecond in th' unfiniſh'd ſong!

Thoſe works divine, which, on his death-bed laid,

To thee, O CRAGGS, th' expiring ſage convey'd,

Great, but ill-omen'd monument of fame,

Nor he ſurviv'd to give, nor thou to claim.

Swift after him thy ſocial ſpirit flies,

And cloſe to his, how ſoon! thy coffin lies.

Bleſt pair! whoſe union future bards ſhall tell

In future tongues; each other's boaſt! farewel.

Farewel! whom join'd in fame, in friendſhip try'd,

No chance could ſever, nor the grave divide.

THE

THE HERMIT.

BY DR. PARNELL.

FAR in a wild, unknown to public view,
From youth to age a reverend Hermit grew;
The mofs his bed, the cave his humble cell,
His food the fruits, his drink the cryftal well:
Remote from man, with God he pafs'd the days,
Prayer all his bufinefs, all his pleafure praife.

A life fo facred, fuch ferene repofe,
Seem'd heaven itfelf, till one fuggeftion rofe—
That vice fhould triumph, virtue vice obey;
This fprung fome doubt of Providence's fway:
His hopes no more a certain profpect boaft,
And all the tenour of his foul is loft.
So when a fmooth expanfe receives impreft
Calm nature's image on its watery breaft,
Down bend the banks, the trees depending grow,
And fkies beneath with anfwering colours glow:

But

But if a ſtone the gentle ſea divide,

Swift ruffling circles curl on every ſide,

And glimmering fragments of a broken ſun;

Banks, trees, and ſkies, in thick diſorder run.

To clear this doubt, to know the world by ſight,

To find if books or ſwains report it right

(For yet by ſwains alone the world he knew,

Whoſe feet came wandering o'er the nightly dew)

He quits his cell; the pilgrim-ſtaff he bore,

And fix'd the ſcallop in his hat before;

Then, with the riſing ſun, a journey went,

Sedate to think, and watching each event.

The morn was waſted in the pathleſs graſs,

And long and loneſome was the wild to paſs;

But when the ſouthern ſun had warm'd the day,

A youth came poſting o'er a croſſing way;

His raiment decent, his complexion fair,

And ſoft in graceful ringlets wav'd his hair:

Then near approaching, Father, hail! he cried;

And hail, my ſon! the reverend Sire replied;

Words

Words follow'd words, from queftion anfwer flow'd,

And talk of various kind deceiv'd the road;

'Till each with other pleas'd, and loth to part,

While in their age they differ, join in heart:

Thus ftands an aged elm in ivy bound,

Thus youthful ivy clafps an elm around.

    Now funk the fun; the clofing hour of day

Came onward, mantled o'er with fober grey;

Nature in filence bid the world repofe;

When near the road a ftately palace rofe:

There by the moon thro' ranks of trees they pafs,

Whofe verdure crown'd their floping fides of grafs.

It chanc'd the noble mafter of the dome

Still made his houfe the wandering ftranger's home:

Yet ftill the kindnefs, from a thirft of praife,

Prov'd the vain flourifh of expenfive eafe.

The pair arrive: the livery'd fervants wait,

Their lord receives them at the pompous gate;

The table groans with coftly piles of food,

And all is more than hofpitably good.

                              Then,

Then, led to reft, the day's long toil they drown,

Deep funk in fleep, and filk, and heaps of down.

At length 'tis morn, and at the dawn of day

Along the wide canals the Zephyrs play;

Frefh o'er the gay parterres the breezes creep,

And fhake the neighbouring wood to banifh fleep:

Up rife the guefts, obedient to the call;

An early banquet deck'd the fplendid hall;

Rich lufcious wine a golden goblet grac'd,

Which the kind mafter forc'd the guefts to tafte.

Then, pleas'd and thankful, from the porch they go;

And, but the Landlord, none had caufe of woe:

His cup was vanifh'd; for in fecret guife

The younger Gueft purloin'd the glittering prize.

As one who fpies a ferpent in his way,

Gliftening and bafking in the fummer ray,

Diforder'd ftops to fhun the danger near,

Then walks with faintnefs on, and looks with fear:

So feem'd the Sire, when, far upon the road,

The fhining fpoil his wiley partner fhow'd.

He

He ſtopp'd with ſilence, walk'd with trembling heart,
And much he wiſh'd, but durſt not aſk, to part:
Murmuring he lifts his eyes, and thinks it hard ,
That generous actions meet a baſe reward.

While thus they paſs, the ſun his glory ſhrouds,
The changing ſkies hang out their ſable clouds;
A ſound in air preſaged approaching rain,
And beaſts to covert ſcud acroſs the plain.
Warn'd by the ſigns, the wandering pair retreat
To ſeek for ſhelter at a neighbouring ſeat:
'Twas built with turrets on a riſing ground,
And ſtrong, and large, and unimprov'd around;
Its owner's temper, timorous and ſevere,
Unkind and griping, caus'd a deſert there.
As near the Miſer's heavy doors they drew,
Fierce riſing guſts with ſudden fury blew,
The nimble lightning mix'd with ſhowers began,
And o'er their heads loud rolling thunder ran.
Here long they knock, but knock or call in vain,
Driven by the wind, and batter'd by the rain.

At

At length fome pity warm'd the mafter's breaft

('Twas then his threfhold firft receiv'd a gueft):

Slow creaking turns the door with jealous care,

And half he welcomes in the fhivering pair;

One frugal faggot lights the naked walls,

And nature's fervour through their limbs recalls:

Bread of the coarfeft fort, with meagre wine,

(Each hardly granted) ferv'd them both to dine;

And when the tempeft firft appear'd to ceafe,

A ready warning bid them part in peace.

    With ftill remark the pondering Hermit view'd,

In one fo rich, a life fo poor and rude;

And why fhould fuch (within himfelf he cried)

Lock the loft wealth a thoufand want befide?

But what new marks of wonder foon take place

In every fettling feature of his face,

When from his veft the young companion bore

That cup the generous landlord own'd before,

And paid profufely with the precious bowl

The ftinted kindnefs of this churlifh foul.

But

But now the clouds in airy tumult fly,

The fun emerging opes an azure fky;

A frefher green the fmelling leaves difplay,

And, glittering as they tremble, cheer the day:

The weather courts them from the poor retreat,

And the glad mafter bolts the wary gate.

While hence they walk, the Pilgrim's bofom wrought

With all the travel of uncertain thought;

His partner's acts without their caufe appear,

'Twas there a vice, and feem'd a madnefs here:

Detefting that, and pitying this, he goes,

Loft and confounded with the various fhows.

Now night's dim fhades again involve the fky; ⎫
Again the wanderers want a place to lie; ⎬
Again they fearch, and find a lodging nigh. ⎭

The foil improv'd around, the manfion neat,

And neither poorly low nor idly great;

It feem'd to fpeak its mafter's turn of mind,

Content, and not to praife, but virtue kind.

Hither

Hither the walkers turn with weary feet,

Then bleſs the manſion, and the maſter greet:

Their greeting fair, beſtow'd with modeſt guiſe,

The courteous maſter hears, and thus replies:

Without a vain, without a grudging heart,

To him, who gives us all, I yield a part;

From him you come, for him accept it here,

A frank and ſober, more than coſtly cheer.

He ſpoke, and bid the welcome table ſpread;

Then talk of virtue till the time of bed;

When the grave houſehold round his hall repair,

Warn'd by a bell, and cloſe the hours with prayer.

At length the world, renew'd by calm repoſe,

Was ſtrong for toil, the dappled morn aroſe;

Before the Pilgrims part, the younger crept

Near the clos'd cradle, where an infant ſlept,

And writh'd his neck: the Landlord's little pride,

O ſtrange return! grew black, and gaſp'd, and died.

Horror of horrors! what! his only ſon!

How look'd our Hermit when the faƈt was done;

Not

Not hell, tho' hell's black jaws in funder part,

And breathe blue fire, could more affault his heart.

Confus'd and ftruck with filence at the deed,

He flies, but trembling fails to fly with fpeed.

His fteps the Youth purfues; the country lay

Perplex'd with roads, a fervant fhow'd the way:

A river crofs'd the path; the paffage o'er

Was nice to find; the fervant trod before;

Long arms of oaks an open bridge fupplied,

And deep the waves beneath the bending glide.

The Youth, who feem'd to watch a time to fin,

Approach'd the carelefs guide, and thruft him in;

Plunging he falls, and rifing lifts his head,

Then flafhing turns, and finks among the dead.

Wild fparkling rage inflames the father's eyes,

He burfts the bands of fear, and madly cries,

Detefted wretch!—But fcarce his fpeech began,

When the ftrange partner feem'd no longer man:

His youthful face grew more ferenely fweet;

His robe turn'd white, and flow'd upon his feet;

Fair rounds of radiant points inveſt his hair;

Celeſtial odours breathe through purpled air;

And wings, whoſe colours glitter'd on the day,

Wide at his back their gradual plumes diſplay.

The form ethereal burſts upon his fight,

And moves in all the majeſty of light.

Tho' loud at firſt the Pilgrim's paſſion grew,

Sudden he gaz'd, and wiſt not what to do;

Surprize in ſecret chains his words ſuſpends,

And in a calm his ſettling temper ends.

But ſilence here the beauteous Angel broke

(The voice of muſic raviſh'd as he ſpoke).

Thy prayer, thy praiſe, thy life to vice unknown,

In ſweet memorial riſe before the throne:

Theſe charms, ſuccefs in our bright region find,

And force an Angel down to calm thy mind;

For this commiſſion'd, I forſook the ſky;

Nay, ceaſe to kneel—thy fellow-ſervant I.

Then know the truth of government divine,

And let theſe ſcruples be no longer thine.

The

The Maker juftly claims that world he made;
In this the right of Providence is laid;
Its facred majefty through all depends
On ufing fecond means to work his ends;
'Tis thus, withdrawn in ftate from human eye,
The Power exerts his attributes on high;
Your actions ufes, nor controuls your will,
And bids the doubting fons of men be ftill.

What ftrange events can ftrike with more furprize,
Than thofe which lately ftruck thy wondering eyes?
Yet, taught by thefe, confefs th' Almighty juft,
And, where you can't unriddle, learn to truft!

The great, vain man, who far'd on coftly food,
Whofe life was too luxurious to be good;
Who made his ivory ftands with goblets fhine,
And forc'd his guefts to morning draughts of wine;
Hath, with the cup, the gracelefs cuftom loft,
And ftill he welcomes, but with lefs of coft.

The mean fufpicious wretch, whofe bolted door
Ne'er mov'd in pity to the wandering poor,

With

With him I left the cup, to teach his mind

That Heaven can bleſs, if mortals will be kind:

Conſcious of wanting worth, he views the bowl,

And feels compaſſion touch his grateful ſoul.

Thus artiſts melt the ſullen ore of lead,

With heaping coals of fire upon its head;

In the kind warmth the metal learns to glow,

And, looſe from droſs, the ſilver runs below.

Long had·our pious friend in virtue trod,

But now·the child half wean'd his heart from God;

(Child of his age) for him he liv'd in pain,

And meaſur'd back his ſteps to earth again.

To what exceſſes had his dotage run!

But God, to ſave the father, took the ſon.

To all but thee in fits he ſeem'd to go;

And 'twas my miniſtry to deal the blow.

The poor fond parent, humbled in the duſt,

Now owns in tears the puniſhment was juſt.

But now had all his fortune felt a wrack,

Had that falſe ſervant ſped in ſafety back;

This

This night his treafur'd heaps he meant to fteal,

And what a fund of charity would fail!

Thus Heaven inftructs thy mind: this trial o'er,

Depart in peace, refign, and fin no more.

On founding pinions here the youth withdrew,

The Sage ftood wondering as the Seraph flew.

Thus look'd Elifha when, to mount on high,

His mafter took the chariot of the fky:

The fiery pomp afcending left the view;

The prophet gaz'd, and wifh'd to follow too.

The bending Hermit here a prayer begun:

Lord! as in heaven, on earth thy will be done!

Then gladly turning, fought his ancient place,

And pafs'd a life of piety and peace.

ON THE DEATH OF DR. PARNELL.

ADDRESSED TO THE EARL OF OXFORD
AND EARL MORTIMER.

BY MR. POPE.

Such were the notes thy once-lov'd Poet fung,
'Till death untimely ftopp'd his tuneful tongue.
Oh juft beheld and loft! admir'd and mourn'd!
With fofteft manners, gentleft arts, adorn'd!
Bleft in each fcience, bleft in every ftrain!
Dear to the Mufe, to HARLEY dear—in vain!

For him, thou oft haft bid the world attend,
Fond to forget the ftatefman in the friend:
For SWIFT and him, defpis'd the farce of ftate,
The fober follies of the wife and great;
Dexterous, the craving, fawning crowd to quit,
And pleas'd to 'fcape from flattery to wit.

Abfent or dead, ftill let a friend be dear,
(A figh the abfent claims, the dead a tear)

Recal

Recal thofe nights that clos'd thy toilfome days,

Still hear thy PARNELL in his living lays:

Who carelefs, now, of intereft, fame, or fate,

Perhaps forgets that OXFORD e'er was great;

Or, deeming meaneft what we greateft call,

Beholds thee glorious only in thy fall.

And fure, if aught beneath the feats divine

Can touch immortals, 'tis a foul like thine:

A foul fupreme, in each hard inftance tried,

Above all pain, all paffion, and all pride,

The rage of power, the blaft of public breath,

The luft of lucre, and the dread of death.

In vain to deferts thy retreat is made;

The Mufe attends thee to the filent fhade:

'Tis her's, the brave man's lateft fteps to trace,

Re-judge his acts, and dignify difgrace;

When intereft calls off all her fneaking train,

When all th' obliged defert, and all the vain,

She waits, or to the fcaffold, or the cell,

When the laft lingering friend hath bid farewell.

E'en

E'en now she shades thy evening-walk with bays,

(No hireling she, no prostitute to praise)

E'en now, observant of the parting ray,

Eyes the calm sun-set of thy various day,

Thro' fortune's cloud one truly great can see,

Nor fears to tell, that Mortimer is he.

THE

THE SPLEEN.

BY MR. *MATTHEW GREEN.*

This motley piece to you I fend,
Who always were a faithful friend;
Who, if difputes fhould happen hence,
Can beft explain the author's fenfe;
And, anxious for the public weal,
Do, what I fing, fo often feel.

The want of method pray excufe,
Allowing for a vapour'd Mufe;
Nor, to a narrow path confin'd,
Hedge in by rules a roving mind.

The child is genuine; you may trace
Throughout the fire's tranfmitted face.
Nothing is ftolen: my Mufe, tho' mean,
Draws from the fpring fhe finds within;
Nor vainly buys what Gildon fells,
Poetic buckets for dry wells.

School-

School-helps I want to climb on high,

Where all the ancient treafures lie,

And there unfeen commit a theft

On wealth, in Greek exchequers left.

Then, where? from whom? what can I fteal,

Who only with the moderns deal?

This were attempting to put on

Raiment from naked bodies won:

They fafely fing before a thief,

They cannot give who want relief;

Some few excepted, names well known,

And juftly laurel'd with renown,

Whofe ftamp of genius marks their ware,

And theft detects: of theft beware;

From Moore fo lafh'd, example fit,

Shun petty larceny in wit.

Firft know, my friend, I do not mean

To write a treatife on the Spleen;

Nor to prefcribe, when nerves convulfe;

Nor mend th' alarum watch, your pulfe:

If

If I am right, your queſtion lay,

What courſe I take to drive away

The day-mare Spleen, by whoſe falſe pleas

Men prove mere ſuicides in eaſe;

And how I do myſelf demean

In ſtormy world to live ſerene.

When by its magic-lantern Spleen

With frightful figures ſpreads life's ſcene,

And threatening proſpects urge my fears,

A ſtranger to the luck of heirs;

Reaſon, ſome quiet to reſtore,

Shews part is ſubſtance, ſhadow more;

With Spleen's dead weight tho' heavy grown,

In life's rough tide I ſink not down,

But ſwim, till Fortune throws a rope,

Buoyant on bladders fill'd with hope.

I always chooſe the plaineſt food

To mend viſcidity of blood.

Hail! water-gruel, healing power,

Of eaſy acceſs to the poor;

Thy

Thy help love's confeffors implore,

And doctors fecretly adore:

To thee I fly, by thee dilute,

Thro' veins my blood doth quicker fhoot,

And by fwift current throws off clean

Prolific particles of Spleen.

I never fick by drinking grow,

Nor keep myfelf a cup too low;

And feldom Chloe's lodgings haunt,

Thrifty of fpirits, which I want.

Hunting I reckon very good

To brace the nerves, and ftir the blood;

But after no field-honours itch,

Atchiev'd by leaping hedge and ditch.

While Spleen lies foft relax'd in bed,

Or o'er coal fires inclines the head,

Hygeia's fons, with hound and horn,

And jovial cry awake the morn:

Thefe fee her from the dufky plight,

Smear'd by th' embraces of the night,

E 4   With

With roral wash redeem her face,

And prove herself of Titan's race;

And, mounting in loose robes the skies,

Shed light and fragrance as she flies:.

Then horse and hound fierce joy display,

Exulting at the Hark-away,

And in pursuit o'er tainted ground

From lungs robust field-notes resound:

Then, as St. George the dragon slew,

Spleen pierc'd, trod down, and dying view;

While all their spirits are on wing,

And woods, and hills, and vallies ring.

    To cure the mind's wrong bias, Spleen,

Some recommend the bowling-green;

Some, hilly walks; all, exercise;

Fling but a stone, the giant dies;

Laugh, and be well.   Monkeys have been

Extreme good doctors for the Spleen;

And kitten, if the humour hit,

Has harlequin'd away the fit.

Since

Since mirth is good in this behalf,

At some particulars let us laugh ;

Witlings, brisk fools, curs'd with half sense,

That stimulates their impotence,

Who buz in rhime, and, like blind flies,

Err with their wings for want of eyes ;

Poor authors worshipping a calf,

Deep tragedies that make us laugh,

A strict dissenter saying grace,

A lecturer preaching for a place,

Folks, things prophetic to dispense,

Making the past the future tense,

The popish dubbing of a priest,

Fine epitaphs on knaves deceas'd,

Green-apron'd Pythonissa's rage,

Great Æsculapius on his stage,

A miser starving to be rich,

The prior of Newgate's dying speech,

A jointur'd widow's ritual state,

Two Jews disputing tête-à-tête,

New

New almanacks compos'd by feers,

Experiments on felons ears,

Difdainful prudes, who ceafelefs ply

The fuperb mufcle of the eye,

A coquet's April-weather face,

A Queenborough Mayor behind his mace,

And fops in military fhew,

Are fovereign for the cafe in view.

 If Spleen-fogs rife at clofe of day,

I clear my evening with a play,

Or to fome concert take my way;

The company, the fhine of lights,

The fcenes of humour, mufic's flights,

Adjuft and fet the foul to rights.

 Life's moving pictures, well-wrought plays,

To others' griefs attention raife:

Here, while the tragic fictions glow,

We borrow joy by pitying woe;

There, gaily comic fcenes delight,

And hold true mirrors to our fight.

Virtue,

Virtue, in charming drefs array'd,

Calling the paffions to her aid,

When moral fcenes juft actions join,

Takes fhape, and fhews her face divine.

Mufic has charms, we all may find,

Ingratiate deeply with the mind.

When art does found's high power advance,

To mufic's pipe the paffions dance ;

Motions unwill'd its powers have fhewn,

Tarantulated by a tune.

Many have held the foul to be

Nearly allied to harmony:

Her have I known, indulging grief,

And fhunning company's relief,

Unveil her face, and looking round

Own, by neglecting forrow's wound,

The confanguinity of found.

In rainy days keep double guard,

Or Spleen will furely be too hard ;

Which,

Which, like thofe fifh by failors met,

Fly higheft, while their wings are wet.

In fuch dull weather, fo unfit

To enterprize a work of wit,

When clouds one yard of azure fky,

That's fit for fimile, deny,

I drefs my face with ftudious looks,

And fhorten tedious hours with books.

But if dull fogs invade the head,

That memory minds not what is read,

I fit in window dry as ark,

And on the drowning world remark:

Or to fome coffee-houfe I ftray

For news, the manna of the day,

And from the hipp'd difcourfes gather,

That politics go by the weather:

Then feek good-humour'd tavern chums,

And play at cards, but for fmall fums;

Or with the merry fellows quaff,

And laugh aloud with them that laugh;

Or

Or drink a joco-ferious cup

With fouls who've ta'en their freedom up;

And let my mind, beguil'd by talk,

In Epicurus' garden walk,

Who thought it heav'n to be ferene;

Pain, hell; and purgatory, Spleen.

    Sometimes I drefs, with women fit,

And chat away the gloomy fit,

Quit the ftiff garb of ferious fenfe,

And wear a gay impertinence;

Nor think, nor fpeak with any pains,

But lay on fancy's neck the reins;

Talk of unufual fwell of waift

In maid of honour loofely lac'd,

And beauty borrowing Spanifh red,

And loving pair with feparate bed,

And jewels pawn'd for lofs of game,

And then redeem'd by lofs of fame;

Of Kitty (aunt left in the lurch

By grave pretence to go to church)

Perceiv'd

Perceiv'd in hack with lover fine,

Like Will. and Mary on the coin:

And thus in modifh manner we

In aid of fugar fweeten tea.

Permit, ye fair, your idol form,

Which e'en the coldeft heart can warm,

May with its beauties grace my line,

While I bow down before its fhrine,

And your throng'd altars with my lays

Perfume, and get by giving praife. .

With fpeech fo fweet, fo fweet a mien,

You excommunicate the Spleen,

Which, fiend-like, flies the magic ring

You form with found, when pleas'd to fing.

Whate'er you fay, howe'er you move,

We look, we liften, and approve.

Your touch, which gives to feeling blifs,

Our nerves officious throng to kifs;

By Celia's pat, on their report,

The grave-air'd foul, inclin'd to fport,

Renounces

Renounces wifdom's fullen pomp,

And loves the floral game, to romp.

For who can view the pointed rays,

That from black eyes fcintillant blaze?

Love on his throne of glory feems

Encompafs'd with fatellite beams.

But when blue eyes, more foftly bright,

Diffufe benignly humid light,

We gaze, and fee the fmiling Loves,

And Cytherea's gentle doves,

And raptur'd fix in fuch a face

Love's mercy-feat, and throne of grace.

Shine but on age, you melt its fnow;

Again fires long-extinguifh'd glow;

And, charm'd by witchery of eyes,

Blood long congealed liquefies:

True miracle, and fairly done

By heads which are ador'd while on.

But Oh! what pity 'tis to find

Such beauties both of form and mind,

By

By modern breeding much debas'd,

In half the female world at leaft!

Hence I with care fuch lotteries fhun,

Where, a prize mifs'd, I'm quite undone;

And han't, by venturing on a wife,

Yet run the greateft rifk in life.

 Mothers, and guardian aunts, forbear

Your impious pains to form the fair;

Nor lay out fo much coft and art

But to deflower the virgin heart;   .

Of every folly-foftering bed

By quickening heat of cuftom bred.

Rather than by your culture fpoil'd,

Defift, and give us nature wild;

Delighted with a hoyden foul,

Which truth and innocence controul.

Coquets, leave off affected arts,

Gay fowlers at a flock of hearts;

Woodcocks to fhun your fnares have fkill,

You fhew fo plain, you ftrive to kill.

In

In love the artlefs catch the game,

And they fcarce mifs who never aim.

The world's great Author did create

The fex to fit the nuptial ftate,

And meant a blefling in a wife

To folace the fatigues of life;

And old infpired times difplay,

How wives could love, and yet obey.

Then truth, and patience of controul,

And houfewife-arts adorn'd the foul;

And charms, the gift of nature, fhone;

And jealoufy, a thing unknown:

Veils were the only mafks they wore;

Novels (receipts to make a whore)

Nor ombre, nor quadrille they knew,

Nor Pam's puiffance felt at loo:

Wife men did not, to be thought gay,

Then compliment their power away:

But left, by frail defires mifled,

The girls forbidden paths fhould tread,

F   Of

Of ignorance rais'd the safe high wall;

We sink haw-haws, that shew them all:

Thus we at once solicit sense,

And charge them not to break the fence.

Now, if untir'd, consider friend,

What I avoid to gain my end.

I never am at Meeting seen,

Meeting, that region of the Spleen;

The broken heart, the busy fiend,

The inward call, on Spleen depend.

Law, licens'd breaking of the peace,

To which vacation is disease,

A gypsy diction scarce known well

By th' magi, who law-fortunes tell,

I shun; nor let it breed within

Anxiety, and that the Spleen;

Law, grown a forest, where perplex

The mazes, and the brambles vex,

Where its twelve verderers every day

Are changing still the public way;

Yet

Yet if we miſs our path and err,

We grievous penalties incur;

And wanderers tire, and tear their ſkin,

And then get out where they went in.

 I never game, and rarely bet;

Am loth to lend, or run in debt:

No compter-writs me agitate,

Who moralizing paſs the gate,

And there mine eyes on ſpendthrifts turn,

Who vainly o'er their bondage mourn:

Wiſdom, before beneath their care,

Pays her upbraiding viſits there;

And forces folly thro' the grate

Her panegyric to repeat:

This view, profuſely when inclin'd,

Enters a caveat in the mind:

Experience, join'd with common ſenſe,

To mortals is a providence.

 Paſſion, as frequently is ſeen,

Subſiding ſettles into Spleen:

Hence,

Hence, as the plague of happy life,

I run away from party-ſtrife ;

A prince's cauſe, a church's claim,

I've known to raiſe a mighty flame,

And prieſt, as ſtoker, very free

To throw in peace and charity.

    That tribe, whoſe practicals decree

Small-beer the deadlieſt hereſy;

Who, fond of pedigree, derive

From the moſt noted whore alive ;

Who own wine's old prophetic aid,

And love the mitre Bacchus made ;

Forbid the faithful to depend

On half-pint drinkers for a friend,

And in whoſe gay red-letter'd face

We read good-living more than grace:

Nor they ſo pure, and ſo preciſe,

Immaculate as their white of eyes,

Who for the ſpirit hug the Spleen,

Phylacter'd throughout all their mien ;

Who

Who their ill-tafted home-brew'd pray'r

To the ftate's mellow forms prefer;

Who doctrines, as infectious, fear,

Which are not fteep'd in vinegar,

And famples of heart-chefted grace

Expofe in fhew-glafs of the face,

Did never me as yet provoke,

Either to honour band and cloak,

Or deck my hat with leaves of oak.

 I rail not with mock-patriot grace

At folks, becaufe they are in place.;

Nor, hir'd to praife with ftallion pen,

Serve the ear-lechery of men;

But to avoid religious jars

The laws are my expofitors,

Which in my doubting mind create

Conformity to church and ftate.

I go, purfuant to my plan,

To Mecca with the caravan;

And

And think it right in common fenfe
Both for diverfion and defence.

　Reforming fchemes are none of mine;
To mend the world's a vaft defign:
Like theirs, who tug in little boat
To pull to them the fhip afloat,
While to defeat their labour'd end,
At once both wind and ftream contend:
Succefs herein is feldom feen,
And zeal, when baffled, turns to Spleen.

　Happy the man, who, innocent,
Grieves not at ills he can't prevent;
His fkiff does with the current glide,
Not puffing pull'd againft the tide;
He, paddling by the fcuffling crowd,
Sees unconcern'd life's wager row'd;
And when he can't prevent foul play,
Enjoys the folly of the fray.

　By thefe refleċtions I repeal
Each hafty promife made in zeal.

When

When general Proclamations fay,

" We are bound our great light to difp'ay,

" And Indian darknefs drive away,"

Yet none but drunken watchmen fend,

And fcoundrel link-boys for that end ;

When they cry up this holy war,

" Which every chriftian fhould be for,"

Yet fuch as owe the law their ears,

We find employ'd as engineers ;

This view my forward zeal fo fhocks,

In vain they hold the money-box :

At fuch a conduct, which intends

By vicious means fuch virtuous ends,

I laugh off Spleen, and keep my penco

From fpoiling Indian innocence.

Yet philofophic love of eafe

I fuffer not to prove difeafe ;

But rife up in the virtuous caufe

Of a free prefs, and equal laws,

The

The prefs reftrain'd! nefandous thought!

In vain our fires have nobly fought:

While free from force the prefs remains,

Virtue and Freedom chear our plains,

And learning largeffes beftows,

And keeps uncenfur'd open houfe.

We to the nation's public mart

Our works of wit, and fchemes of art,

And philofophic goods this way,

Like water-carriage, cheap convey.

This tree, which knowledge fo affords,

Inquifitors with flaming fwords

From lay-approach with zeal defend,

Left their own paradife fhould end.

The prefs from her fecundous womb

Brought forth the arts of Greece and Rome;

Her offspring, fkill'd in logic war,

Truth's banner wav'd in open air;

The monfter Superftition fled,

And hid in fhades its Gorgon head;

And

And lawlefs power, the long-kept field,

By reafon quell'd, was forc'd to yield.

This nurfe of arts, and freedom's fence

To chain, is treafon againft fenfe;

And Liberty, thy thoufand tongues

None filence, who defign no wrongs;

For thofe, that ufe the gag's reftraint,

Firft rob, before they ftop complaint.

Since difappointment galls within,

And fubjugates the foul to Spleen,

Moft fchemes, as money-fnares, I hate,

And bite not at projector's bait;

Sufficient wrecks appear each day,

And yet frefh fools are caft away.

Ere well the bubbled can turn round,

Their painted veffel runs aground;

Or in deep feas it overfets

By a fierce hurricane of debts;

Or helm-directors in one trip,

Freight firft embezzled, fink the fhip.

Such

Such was of late a corporation,

The brazen ferpent of the nation,

Which, when hard accidents diftrefs'd,

The poor muft look at to be bleft,

And thence expect, with paper feal'd

By fraud and ufury, to be heal'd.

   I in no foul-confumption wait

Whole years at levees of the great;

And hungry hopes regale the while

On the fpare diet of a fmile:

There you may fee the idol ftand

With mirror in his wanton hand;

Above, below, now here, now there

He throws about the funny glare:

Crowds pant, and prefs to feize the prize,

The gay delufion of their eyes.

   When Fancy tries her limning fkill

To draw and colour at her will,

And raife and round the figures well,

And fhew her talent to excel,

I guard

I guard my heart, left it fhould woo

Unreal beauties fancy drew,

And difappointed, feel defpair

At lofs of things that never were.

When I lean politicians mark

Grazing on æther in the park;

Who e'er on wing with open throats

Fly at debates, expreffes, votes,

Juft in the manner fwallows ufe,

Catching their airy food of news;

Whofe latrant ftomachs oft moleft

The deep-laid plans their dreams fuggeft:

Or fee fome poet penfive fit,

Fondly miftaking Spleen for Wit;

Who, tho' fhort-winded, ftill will aim

To found the epic trump of Fame;

Who ftill on Phœbus' fmiles will doat,

Nor learn conviction from his coat;

I blefs my ftars, I never knew

Whimfeys, which clofe purfu'd, undo,

And

And have from old experience been

Both parent and the child of Spleen.

Thefe fubjects of Apollo's ftate,

Who from falfe fire derive their fate,

With airy purchafes undone

Of lands, which none lend money on,

Born dull, had follow'd thriving ways,

Nor loft one hour to gather bays:

Their fancies firft delirious grew,

And fcenes ideal took for true.

Fine to the fight Parnaffus lies,

And with falfe profpects cheats their eyes;

The fabled gods the poets fing,

A feafon of perpetual fpring,

Brooks, flowery fields, and groves of trees,

Affording fweets and fimiles,

Gay dreams infpir'd in myrtle bowers,

And wreaths of undecaying flowers,

Apollo's harp with airs divine,

The facred mufic of the Nine,

Views

Views of the temple rais'd to Fame,

And for a vacant nitch proud aim,

Ravifh their fouls, and plainly fhew

What Fancy's fketching power can do:

They will attempt the mountain fteep,

Where on the top, like dreams in fleep,

The Mufes revelations fhew,

That find men crack'd, or make them fo.

    You friend, like me, the trade of rhime

Avoid, elaborate wafte of time;

Nor are content to be undone,

To pafs for Phœbus' crazy fon.

Poems, the hop-grounds of the brain,

Afford the moft uncertain gain;

And lotteries never tempt the wife

With blanks fo many to a prize.

I only tranfient vifits pay,

Meeting the Mufes in my way,

Scarce known to the faftidious dames,

Nor fkill'd to call them by their names.

Nor

Nor can their paſſports in theſe days,

Your profit warrant, or your praiſe.

On poems by their dictates writ,

Critics, as ſworn appraiſers, ſit,

And, mere upholſterers, in a trice

On gems and paintings ſet a price.

Theſe tayloring artiſts for our lays

Invent crampt rules, and, with ſtrait ſtays

Striving free Nature's ſhape to hit,

Emaciate ſenſe, before they fit.

A common place, and many friends,

Can ſerve the plagiary's ends;

Whoſe eaſy vamping talent lies,

Firſt wit to pilfer, then diſguiſe.

Thus ſome, devoid of art and ſkill

To ſearch the mine on Pindus' hill,

Proud to aſpire and workmen grow,

By genius doom'd to ſtay below,

For their own digging ſhew the town

Wit's treaſure brought by others down.

Some

Some wanting, if they find a mine,

An artiſt's judgment to refine,

On fame precipitately fix'd,

The ore with baſer metals mix'd

Melt down, impatient of delay,

And call the vicious maſs a play :

All theſe engage, to ſerve their ends,

A band ſelect of truſty friends,

Who, leſſon'd right, extol the thing,

As Pſapho taught his birds to ſing,

Then to the ladies they ſubmit,

Returning officers on wit ;

A crowded houſe their preſence draws,

And on the beaus impoſes laws ;

A judgment in its favour ends,

When all the pannel are its friends :

Their natures merciful and mild

Have from mere pity ſav'd the child ;

In bulruſh ark the bantling found,

Helpleſs and ready to be drown'd,

They

They have preferv'd by kind fupport,

And brought the baby-mufe to court.

But there's a youth, that you can name,

Who needs no leading-ftrings to fame,

Whofe quick maturity of brain

The birth of Pallas may explain:

Dreaming of whofe depending fate,

I heard Melpomene debate,

" This, this is he, that was foretold

Should emulate our Greeks of old;

Infpir'd by me with facred art,

He fings, and rules the varied heart;

If Jove's dread anger he rehearfe,

We hear the thunder in his verfe;

If he defcribes love turn'd to rage,

The furies riot in his page;

If he fair liberty and law

By ruffian power expiring draw,

The keener paffions then engage

Aright, and fanctify their rage;

If

If he attempt difaftrous love,
We hear thofe plaints that wound the grove,
Within, the kinder paffions glow,
And tears diftill'd from pity flow."

From the bright vifion I defcend,
And my deferted theme attend.

Me never did ambition feize,
Strange fever, moft inflam'd by eafe!
The active lunacy of pride,
That courts jilt Fortune for a bride;
This paradife-tree, fo fair and high,
I view with no afpiring eye:
Like afpine fhake the reftlefs leaves,
And Sodom-fruit our pains deceives;
Whence frequent falls give no furprize,
But fits of Spleen call'd " growing wife."
Greatnefs in glittering forms difplay'd
Affects weak eyes much us'd to fhade;
And by its falfly-envy'd fcene
Gives felf-debafing fits of Spleen.

We

We fhould be pleas'd that things are fo,

Who do for nothing fee the fhow,

And, middle-fiz'd, can pafs between

Life's hubbub fafe, becaufe unfeen;

And 'midft the glare of greatnefs trace

A watery fun-fhine in the face;

And pleafures fled to, to redrefs

The fad fatigue of idlenefs.

 Contentment, parent of delight,

So much a ftranger to our fight,

Say, goddefs, in what happy place

Mortals behold thy blooming face;

Thy gracious aufpices impart,

And for thy temple chufe my heart.

They, whom thou deigneft to infpire,

Thy fcience learn, to bound defire;

By happy alchymy of mind

They turn to pleafure all they find;

They both difdain an outward mien,

The grave and folemn garb of Spleen,

And

And meretricious arts of drefs,

To feign a joy, and hide diftrefs;

Unmov'd when the rude tempeft blows,

Without an opiate they repofe;

And cover'd by your fhield, defy

The whizzing fhafts, that round them fly:

Nor, meddling with the gods' affairs,

Concern themfelves with diftant cares;

But place their blifs in mental reft,

And feaft upon the good poffefs'd.

Forc'd by foft violence of prayer,

The blythfome goddefs fooths my care;

I feel the deity infpire,

And thus fhe models my defire:

Two hundred pounds, half-yearly paid,

Annuity fecurely made;

A farm fome twenty miles from town,

Small, tight, falubrious, and my own;

Two maids, that never faw the town,

A ferving-man not quite a clown;

A boy

A boy to help to tread the mow,

And drive, while t'other holds the plough;

A chief of temper form'd to pleafe,

Fit to converfe, and keep the keys;

And better to preferve the peace,

Commiffion'd by the name of niece:

With underftandings of a fize

To think their mafter very wife.

May Heaven (it's all I wifh for) fend

One genial room to treat a friend;

Where decent cupboard, little plate,

Difplay benevolence, not ftate.

And may my humble dwelling ftand

Upon fome chofen fpot of land;

A pond before full to the brim,

Where cows may cool, and geefe may fwim;

Behind, a green like velvet neat,

Soft to the eye, and to the feet;

Where odorous plants in evening fair

Breathe all around ambrofial air;

From

From Eurus, foe to kitchen-ground,

Fenc'd by a flope with bufhes crown'd,

Fit dwelling for the feather'd throng,

Who pay their quit-rents with a fong;

With opening views of hill and dale,

Which fenfe and fancy too regale,

Where the half-cirque, which vifion bounds,

Like amphitheatre furrounds:

And woods impervious to the breeze,

Thick phalanx of embodied trees,

From hills thro' plains in dufk array

Extended far, repel the day.

Here ftillnefs, height, and folemn fhade

Invite, and contemplation aid:

Here nymphs from hollow oaks relate

The dark decrees and will of fate;

And dreams beneath the fpreading beech

Infpire, and docile fancy teach,

While foft as breezy breath of wind,

Impulfes ruftle thro' the mind:

Here

Here Dryads, fcorning Phœbus' ray,

While Pan melodious pipes away,

In meafur'd motions frifk about,

'Till old Silenus puts them out.

There fee the clover, pea, and bean,

Vie in variety of green;

Frefh paftures fpeckled o'er with fheep,

Brown fields their fallow fabbaths keep,

Plump Ceres golden treffes wear,

And poppy top-knots deck her hair;

And filver ftreams through meadows ftray,

And Naiads on the margin play,

And leffer nymphs on fide of hills

From play-thing urns pour down the rills.

    Thus fhelter'd, free from care and ftrife,

May I enjoy a calm thro' life:

See faction, fafe in low degree,

As men at land fee ftorms at fea;

And laugh at miferable elves,

Not kind, fo much as to themfelves;

Curs'd

Curs'd with fuch fouls of bafe alloy,

As can poffefs, but not enjoy;

Debarr'd the pleafure to impart

By avarice, fphincter of the heart;

Who wealth, hard earn'd by guilty cares,

Bequeath untouch'd to thanklefs heirs.

May I, with look ungloom'd by guile,

And wearing Virtue's livery-fmile,

Prone the diftreffed to relieve,

And little trefpaffes forgive,

With income not in Fortune's pow'r,

And fkill to make a bufy hour,

With trips to town life to amufe,

. To purchafe books, and hear the news,

To fee old friends, brufh off the clown,

And quicken tafte at coming down,

Unhurt by ficknefs' blafting rage,

And flowly mellowing in age,

When Fate extends its gathering gripe,

Fall off like fruit grown fully ripe,

Quit

Quit a worn being without pain ;

Perhaps to bloſſom ſoon again !

But now more ſerious ſee me grow,

And what I think, my Memmius, know.

Th' enthuſiaſt's hopes, and raptures wild,

Have never yet my reaſon foil'd ;

His ſpringy ſoul dilates like air,

When free from weight of ambient care,

And, huſh'd in meditation deep,

Slides into dreams, as when aſleep ;

Then, fond of new diſcoveries grown,

Proves a Columbus of her own ;

Diſdains the narrow bounds of place,

And thro' the wilds of endleſs ſpace,

Born up on metaphyſick wings,

Chaſes light forms and ſhadowy things,

And in the vague excurſion caught,

Brings home ſome rare exotick thought.

The melancholy man ſuch dreams,

As brighteſt evidence, eſteems ;

Fain

Fain would he fee fome diftant fcene

Suggefted by his reftlefs Spleen,

And Fancy's telefcope applies

With tinctur'd glafs to cheat his eyes.

Such thoughts, as love the gloom of night,

I clofe examine by the light;

For who, tho' brib'd by gain to lie,

Dare fun-beam-written truths deny,

And execute plain common fenfe

On faith's mere hearfay evidence?

That fuperftition mayn't create,

And club its ill with thofe of fate,

I many a notion take to tafk,

Made dreadful by its vifor-mafk;

Thus fcruple, fpafm of the mind,

Is cur'd, and certainty I find;

Since optic reafon fhews me plain,

I dreaded fpectres of the brain;

And legendary fears are gone,

Tho' in tenacious childhood fown.

Thus

Thus in opinions I commence
Freeholder in the proper fenfe;
And neither fuit nor fervice do,
Nor homage to pretenders fhew,
Who boaft themfelves by fpurious roll
Lords of the manor of the foul:
Preferring fenfe, from chin that's bare,
To nonfenfe thron'd in whifker'd hair.

    To thee, Creator uncreate,
O Entium Ens! divinely great!—
Hold, Mufe, nor melting pinions try,
Nor near the blazing glory fly,
Nor ftraining break thy feeble bow,
Unfeather'd arrows far to throw:
Thro' fields unknown nor madly ftray,
Where no ideas mark the way:
With tender eyes, and colours faint,
And trembling hands forbear to paint:
Who features veil'd by light can hit?
Where can, what has no outline, fit?

                              My

My foul, the vain attempt forego;

Thyfelf, the fitter fubject, know.

He wifely fhuns the bold extreme,

Who foon lays by th' unequal theme,

Nor runs, with wifdom's Sirens caught,

On quickfands fwallowing fhipwreck'd thought;

But, confcious of his diftance, gives

Mute praife, and humble negatives.

In one, no object of our fight,

Immutable and infinite,

Who can't be cruel, or unjuft,

Calm and refign'd, I fix my truft;

To him my paft and prefent ftate

I owe, and muft my future fate.

A ftranger into life I'm come,

Dying may be our going home;

Tranfported here by angry Fate,

The convicts of a prior ftate.

Hence

Hence I no anxious thoughts beſtow

On matters, I can never know;

Thro' life's foul way, like vagrant paſs'd,

He'll grant a ſettlement at laſt,

And with ſweet eaſe the wearied crown,

By leave to lay his being down.

If doom'd to dance th' eternal round

Of life no ſooner loſt but found,

And diſſolution ſoon to come,

Like ſponge, wipes out life's preſent ſum,

But can't our ſtate of power bereave

An endleſs ſeries to receive;

Then, if hard dealt with here by fate,

We balance in another ſtate,

(And conſciouſneſs muſt go along

And ſign th' acquittance for the wrong)

He for his creatures muſt decree

More happineſs than miſery,

Or

Or be fuppofed to create,

Curious to try, what 'tis to hate:

And do an act, which rage infers,

'Caufe lamenefs halts, or blindnefs errs.

Thus, thus I fteer my bark, and fail

On even keel with gentle gale;

At helm I make my reafon fit,

My crew of paffions all fubmit.

If dark and bluftering prove fome nights,

Philofophy puts forth her lights;

Experience holds the cautious glafs,

To fhun the breakers as I pafs,

And frequent throws the wary lead,

To fee what dangers may be hid:

And once in feven years I'm feen

At Bath or Tunbridge, to careen;

Tho' pleas'd to fee the dolphins play,

I mind my compafs and my way;

With

With ſtore ſufficient for relief,

And wiſely ſtill prepar'd to reef;

Nor wanting the diſperſive bowl

Of cloudy weather in the ſoul,

I make (may Heaven propitious ſend

Such wind and weather to the end !)

Neither becalm'd, nor over-blown,

Life's voyage to the world unknown

THE

THE FLOWER AND THE LEAF.

BY DRYDEN.

Now turning from the wintry figns, the fun
His courfe exalted thro' the Ram had run,
And, whirling up the fkies, his chariot drove
Thro' Taurus, and the lightfome realms of love;
Where Venus from her orb defcends in fhowers,
To glad the ground, and paint the fields with flowers;
When firft the tender blades of grafs appear,
And buds, that yet the blaft of Eurus fear,
Stand at the door of life, and doubt to clothe the year;
Till gentle heat, and foft repeated rains,
Make the green blood to dance within their veins;
Then, at their call, embolden'd out they come,
And fwell the gems, and burft the narrow room;
Broader and broader yet their blooms difplay,
Salute the welcome fun, and entertain the day.

Then

Then from their breathing fouls the fweets repair

To fcent the fkies, and purge th' unwholfome air:

Joy fpreads the heart, and, with a general fong,

Spring iffues out, and leads the jolly months along.

 In that fweet feafon, as in bed I lay,

And fought in fleep to pafs the night away,

I turn'd my wearied fide, but ftill in vain,

Tho' full of youthful health and void of pain:

Cares I had none, to keep me from my reft,

For love had never enter'd in my breaft;

I wanted nothing fortune could fupply,

Nor did fhe flumber till that hour deny:

I wonder'd then, but after found it true,

Much joy had dried away the balmy dew;

Seas would be pools, without the brufhing air,

To curl the waves; and fure fome little care

Should weary nature fo, to make her want repair.

 When Chanticleer the fecond watch had fung,

Scorning the fcorner fleep, from bed I fprung;

And

And dreffing, by the moon, in loofe array,

Pafs'd out in open air, preventing day,

And fought a goodly grove, as fancy led my way.

Straight as a line in beauteous order ftood

Of oaks unfhorn a venerable wood;

Frefh was the grafs beneath, and every tree,

At diftance planted in a due degree,

Their branching arms in air with equal fpace

Stretch'd to their neighbours with a long embrace;

And the new leaves on every bough were feen,

Some ruddy colour'd, fome of lighter green:

The painted birds, companions of the fpring,

Hopping from fpray to fpray, were heard to fing:

Both eyes and ears receiv'd a like delight,

Enchanting mufic, and a charming fight.

On Philomel I fix'd my whole defire;

And liften'd for the queen of all the quire;

Fain would I hear her heavenly voice to fing;

And wanted yet an omen to the fpring.

H   Attending

Attending long in vain, I took the way,

Which thro' a path, but fcarcely printed, lay;

In narrow mazes oft it feem'd to meet,

And look'd, as lightly prefs'd by fairy feet.

Wandering I walk'd alone, for ftill methought

To fome ftrange end fo ftrange a path was wrought:

At laft it led me where an arbour ftood,

The facred receptacle of the wood:

This place unmark'd, tho' oft I walk'd the green,

In all my progrefs I had never feen:

And feiz'd at once with wonder and delight,

Gaz'd all around me, new to the tranfporting fight.

'Twas bench'd with turf, and goodly to be feen,

The thick young grafs arofe in frefher green:

The mound was newly made, no fight could pafs

Betwixt the nice partitions of the grafs;

The well-united fods fo clofely lay;

And all around the fhades defended it from day:

For fycamores with eglantine were fpread,

A hedge about the fides, a covering over head.

And

And fo the fragrant brier was wove between,

The fycamore and flowers were mixt with green,

That nature feem'd to vary the delight;

And fatisfy'd at once the fmell and fight.

The mafter workman of the bower was known

Through fairy-lands, and built for Oberon;

Who twining leaves with fuch proportion drew,

They rofe by meafure, and by rule they grew;

No mortal tongue can half the beauty tell;

For none but hands divine could work fo well.

Both roof and fides were like a parlour made,

A foft recefs, and a cool fummer fhade;

The hedge was fet fo thick, no foreign eye

The perfons plac'd within it could efpy;

But all that pafs'd without with eafe was feen,

As if nor fence nòr tree was plac'd between:

'Twas border'd with a field; and fome was plain

With grafs, and fome was fow'd with rifing grain:

That, now the dew with fpangles deck'd the ground,

A fweeter fpot of earth was never found.

I look'd

I look'd and look'd, and ftill with new delight;

Such joy my foul, fuch pleafures fill'd my fight;

And the frefh eglantine exhal'd a breath,

Whofe odours were of power to raife from death.

Nor fullen difcontent, nor anxious care,

Ev'n tho' brought thither, could inhabit there:

But thence they fled, as from their mortal foe, .

For this fweet place could only pleafure know.

   Thus as I mus'd I caft afide my eye,

And faw a medlar-tree was planted nigh:

The fpreading branches made a goodly fhow,

And full of opening blooms was every bough:

A goldfinch there I faw with gaudy pride

Of painted plumes, that hopp'd from fide to fide,

Still pecking as fhe pafs'd; and ftill fhe drew

The fweets from every flower, and fuck'd the dew:

Suffic'd at length, fhe warbled in her throat,

And tun'd her voice to many a merry note;

But indiftinct, and neither fweet nor clear,

Yet fuch as footh'd my foul, and pleas'd my ear.

Her

Her fhort performance was no fooner try'd,

When fhe I fought, the nightingale, reply'd:

So fweet, fo fhrill, fo varioufly fhe fung,

That the grove echo'd, and the valleys rung:

And I fo ravifh'd with her heavenly note,

I ftood entranc'd, and had no room for thought,

But all o'er-power'd with ecftafy of blifs,

Was in a pleafing dream of paradife;

At length I wak'd, and looking round the bow'r

Search'd every tree, and pry'd on every flower,

If any where by chance I might efpy

The rural poet of the melody;

For ftill methought fhe fung not far away;

At laft I found her on a laurel fpray:

Clofe by my fide fhe fat, and fair in fight,

Full in a line, againft her oppofite;

Where ftood with eglantine the laurel twin'd,

And both their native fweets were well conjoin'd.

On the green bank I fat, and liften'd long;

(Sitting was more convenient for the fong:)

H 3   Nor

Nor till her lay was ended could I move,

But wifh'd to dwell for ever in the grove;

Only methought the time too fwiftly pafs'd,

And every note I fear'd would be the laft:

My fight and fmell, and hearing were employ'd,

And all three fenfes in full guft enjoy'd.

And what alone did all the reft furpafs,

The fweet poffeffion of the fairy place;

Single, and confcious to myfelf alone

Of pleafures to the excluded world unknown:

Pleafures which no where elfe were to be found,

And all Elyfium in a fpot of ground.

 Thus while I fat intent to fee and hear,

And drew perfumes of more than vital air,

All fuddenly I heard the approaching found

Of vocal mufic, on the enchanted ground:

An hoft of faints it feem'd, fo full the quire;

As if the blefs'd above did all confpire

To join their voices, and neglect the lyre.

At length there iffued from the grove behind

A fair affembly of the female kind:

A train lefs fair, as ancient fathers tell,

Seduc'd the fons of heaven to rebel.

I pafs their form, and every charming grace;

Lefs than an angel would their worth debafe:

But their attire, like liveries of a kind,

All rich and rare, is frefh within my mind.

In velvet white as fnow the troop was gown'd,

The feams with fparkling emeralds fet around:

Their hoods and fleeves the fame; and purfled o'er

With diamonds, pearls, and all the fhining ftore

Of Eaftern pomp: their long defcending train,

With rubies edg'd, and faphires, fwept the plain:

High on their heads, with jewels richly fet,

Each lady wore a radiant coronet.

Beneath the circles, all the quire was grac'd

With chaplets green on their fair foreheads plac'd;

Of laurel fome, of woodbine many more;

And wreaths of Agnus-caftus others bore;

Thefe

Thefe laft, who with thofe virgin crowns were drefs'd,

Appear'd in higher honour than the reft :

They danc'd around; but in the midft was feen

A lady of a more majeftic mien;

By ftature and by beauty mark'd their fovereign queen.

   She in the midft began with fober grace;

Her fervants' eyes were fix'd upon her face,

And, as fhe mov'd or turn'd, her motions view'd,

Her meafures kept, and ftep by ftep purfued.

Methought fhe trod the ground with greater grace,

With more of godhead fhining in her face;

And as in beauty fhe furpafs'd the quire,

So, nobler than the reft, was her attire.

A crown of ruddy gold inclos'd her brow,

Plain without pomp, and rich without a fhow:

A branch of Agnus-caftus in her hand

She bore aloft (her fceptre of command;)

Admir'd, ador'd by all the circling crowd,

For wherefoe'er fhe turn'd her face, they bow'd:

And,

And, as she danc'd, a roundelay she sung,

In honour of the laurel, ever young:

She rais'd her voice on high, and sung so clear,

The fawns came scudding from the groves to hear:

And all the bending forest lent an ear.

At every close she made, the attending throng

Reply'd, and bore the burden of the song:

So just, so small, yet in so sweet a note,

It seem'd the music melted in the throat.

   Thus dancing on, and singing as they danc'd,

They to the middle of the mead advanc'd,

Till round my arbour a new ring they made,

And footed it about the secret shade.

O'erjoy'd to see the jolly troop so near,

But somewhat aw'd, I shook with holy fear;

Yet not so much but that I noted well

Who did the most in song or dance excel.

   Not long I had observ'd, when from afar

I heard a sudden symphony of war;

The

The neighing courfers, and the foldiers cry,

And founding trumps that feem'd to tear the fky:

I faw foon after this, behind the grove

From whence the ladies did in order move,

Come iffuing out in arms a warrior train,

That like a deluge pour'd upon the plain;

On barbed fteeds they rode in proud array,

Thick as the college of the bees in May,

When fwarming o'er the dufky fields they fly,

New to the flowers, and intercept the fky:

So fierce they drove, their courfers were fo fleet,

That the turf trembled underneath their feet.

To tell their coftly furniture were long,

The fummer's day would end before the fong:

To purchafe but the tenth of all their ftore

Would make the mighty Perfian monarch poor:

Yet what I can, I will:—Before the reft

The trumpets iffued, in white mantles drefs'd:

A numerous

A numerous troop, and all their heads around

With chaplets green of cerrial-oak were crown'd,

And at each trumpet was a banner bound;

Which waving in the wind difplay'd at large

Their mafter's coat of arms, and knightly charge.

Broad were the banners, and of fnowy hue,

A purer web the filk-worm never drew.

The chief about their necks the fcutcheons wore,

With orient pearls and jewels powder'd o'er :

Broad were their collars too, and every one

Was fet about with many a coftly ftone.

Next thefe, of kings at arms a goodly train

In proud array came prancing o'er the plain :

Their cloaks were cloth of filver mix'd with gold,

And garlands green around their temples roll'd :

Rich crowns were on their royal fcutcheons plac'd,

With fapphires, diamonds, and with rubies grac'd :

And as the trumpets their appearance made,

So thefe in habits were alike array'd;

But

But with a pace more fober, and more flow;

And twenty, rank in rank, they rode a row.

The purfuivants came next, in number more;

And like the heralds each his fcutcheon bore:

Clad in white velvet all their troop they led,

With each an oaken chaplet on his head.

Nine royal knights in equal rank fucceed,

Each warrior mounted on a fiery fteed:

In golden armour glorious to behold;

The rivets of their arms were nail'd with gold.

Their furcoats of white ermine fur were made,

With cloth of gold between, that caft a glittering fhade;

The trappings of their fteeds were of the fame;

The golden fringe ev'n fet the ground on flame,

And drew a precious trail: a crown divine

Of laurel did about their temples twine.

Three henchmen were for every knight affign'd,

All in rich livery clad, and of a kind;

White velvet, but unfhorn, for cloaks they wore;

And each within his hand a truncheon bore:

The

The foremoft held a helm of rare device;
A prince's ranfom would not pay the price.
The fecond bore the buckler of his knight,
The third of cornel-wood a fpear upright,
Headed with piercing fteel, and polifh'd bright.
Like to their lords their equipage was feen,
And all their foreheads crown'd with garlands green.

  And after thefe came arm'd with fpear and fhield
An hoft fo great, as cover'd all the field:
And all their foreheads, like the knights before,
With laurels ever-green were fhaded o'er,
Or oak, or other leaves of lafting kind,
Tenacious of the ftem, and firm againft the wind.
Some in their hands, befide the lance and fhield,
The boughs of woodbine or of hawthorn held,
Or branches for their myftic emblems took,
Of palm, of laurel, or of cerrial-oak.
Thus marching to the trumpet's lofty found
Drawn in two lines adverfe they wheel'd around,
And in the middle meadow took their ground.

Among

Among themfelves the tourney they divide,

In equal fquadrons rang'd on either fide:

Then turn'd their horfes' heads, and man to man,

And fteed to fteed oppos'd, the jufts began.

They lightly fet their lances in the reft,

And, at the fign, againft each other prefs'd:

They met.   I fitting at my eafe beheld

The mix'd events, and fortunes of the field.

Some broke their fpears, fome tumbled horfe and man,

And round the field the lighten'd courfers ran.

An hour and more, like tides, in equal fway

They rufh'd, and won by turns, and loft the day:

At length the nine (who ftill together held)

Their fainting foes to fhameful flight compell'd,

And with refiftlefs force o'er-ran the field.

Thus, to their fame, when finifh'd was the fight,

The victors from their lofty fteeds alight:

Like them difmounted all the warlike train,

And two by two proceeded o'er the plain:

'Till

'Till to the fair affembly they advanc'd,

Who near the fecret arbour fung and danc'd.

The ladies left their meafures at the fight,

To meet the chiefs, returning from the fight,

And each with open arms embrac'd her chofen knight.

Amid the plain a fpreading laurel ftood,

The grace and ornament of all the wood:

That pleafing fhade they fought, a foft retreat

From fudden April fhowers, a fhelter from the heat:

Her leafy arms with fuch extent were fpread,

So near the clouds was her afpiring head,

That hofts of birds, that wing the liquid air,

Perch'd in the boughs, had nightly lodging there:

And flocks of fheep beneath the fhade, from far

Might hear the rattling hail, and wintery war;

From heaven's inclemency here find retreat,

Enjoy the cool, and fhun the fcorching heat:

A hundred knights might there at eafe abide;

And every knight a lady by his fide:

The

The trunk itſelf ſuch odours did bequeath,

That a Moluccan breeze to theſe was common breath.

The lords and ladies here, approaching, paid

Their homage, with a low obeiſance made;

And ſeem'd to venerate the ſacred ſhade.

Theſe rites perform'd, their pleaſures they purſue,

With ſongs of love, and mix with pleaſures new;

Around the holy tree their dance they frame,

And every champion leads his choſen dame.

I caſt my ſight upon the farther field,

And a freſh object of delight beheld:

For from the region of the Weſt I heard

New muſic ſound, and a new troop appear'd,

Of knights and ladies mix'd, a jolly band,

But all on foot they march'd, and hand in hand;

The ladies dreſs'd in rich ſymars were ſeen

Of Florence ſattin, flower'd with white and green,

And for a ſhade betwixt the bloomy gridelin.

The borders of their petticoats below

Were guarded thick with rubies on a row;

And

And every damſel wore upon her head

Of flowers a garland, blended white and red.

Attir'd in mantles all the knights were ſeen,

That gratify'd the view with chearful green:

Their chaplets of their ladies colours were,

Compos'd of white and red, to ſhade their ſhining hair.

Before the merry troop the minſtrels play'd;

All in their maſter's liveries were array'd,

And clad in green, and on their temples wore

The chaplets white and red their ladies bore.

Their inſtruments were various in their kind,

Some for the bow, and ſome for breathing wind:

The ſawtry, pipe, and hautboy's noiſy band,

And the ſoft lute, trembling beneath the touching hand.

A tuft of daiſies on a flowery lay

They ſaw, and thitherward they bent their way;

To this both knights and dames their homage made,

And due obeiſance to the daiſy paid.

And then the band of flutes began to play,

To which a lady ſung a virelay:

I   And

And ftill at every clofe fhe would repeat
The burden of the fong, " The daify is fo fweet."
" The daify is fo fweet," when fhe begun,
The troop of knights and dames continued on :
The concert and the voice fo charm'd my ear,
And footh'd my foul, that it was heaven to hear.

But foon their pleafure pafs'd : at noon of day
The fun with fultry beams began to play :
Not Sirius fhoots a fiercer flame from high,
When with his poifonous breath he blafts the fky :
Then droop'd the fading flowers (their beauty fled)⎫
And clos'd their fickly eyes, and hung the head ;⎬
And rivell'd up with heat, lay dying in their bed.⎭
The ladies gafp'd, and fcarcely could refpire ;
The breath they drew, no longer air, but fire ;
The fainty knights were fcorch'd; and knew not where
To run for fhelter, for no fhade was near ;
And after this the gathering clouds amain
Pour'd down a ftorm of rattling hail and rain :

And

And lightening flafh'd betwixt: the field, and flowers,

Burnt up before, were buried in the fhowers.

The ladies and the knights, no fhelter nigh,

Bare to the weather and the wintery fky,

Were dropping wet, difconfolate and wan,

And thro' their thin array receiv'd the rain;

While thofe in white, protected by the tree,

Saw pafs in vain the affault, and ftood from danger free.

But as compaffion mov'd their gentle minds,

When ceas'd the ftorm, and filent were the winds,

Difpleas'd at what, not fuffering, they had feen,

They went to chear the faction of the green:

The queen in white array, before her band,

Saluting, took her rival by the hand;

So did the knights and dames, with courtly grace,

And with behaviour fweet, their foes embrace.

Then thus the queen with laurel on her brow,

Fair fifter, I have fuffer'd in your woe;

Nor fhall be wanting aught within my power

For your relief in my refrefhing bower.

I 2   That

That other anſwer'd with a lowly look,

And ſoon the gracious invitation took:

For ill at eaſe both ſhe and all her train

The ſcorching ſun had borne, and beating rain.

Like courteſy was us'd by all in white,

Each dame a dame receiv'd, and every knight a knight.

The laurel champions with their ſwords invade

The neighbouring foreſts where the juſts were made,

And ſerewood from the rotten hedges took,

And ſeeds of latent fire from flints provoke:

A chearful blaze aroſe, and by the fire

They warm'd their frozen feet, and dry'd their wet
　　attire.

Refreſh'd with heat, the ladies ſought around

For virtuous herbs, which gather'd from the ground,

They ſqueez'd the juice, and cooling ointment made,

Which on their ſun-burnt cheeks, and their chapt
　　ſkins they laid:

Then ſought green ſalads, which they bade them eat,

A ſovereign remedy for inward heat.

　　　　　　　　　　　　　　　　The

The lady of the leaf ordain'd a feaft,

And made the lady of the flower her gueft:

When lo, a bower afcended on the plain,

With fudden feats ordain'd, and large for either train.

This bower was near my pleafant arbour plac'd,

That I could hear and fee whatever pafs'd:

The ladies fat with each a knight between,

Diftinguifh'd by their colours, white and green;

The vanquifh'd party with the victors join'd,

Nor wanted fweet difcourfe, the banquet of the mind.

Mean time the minftrels play'd on either fide,

Vain of their art, and for the maftery vy'd.

The fweet contention lafted for an hour,

And reach'd my fecret arbour from the bower.

The fun was fet; and Vefper, to fupply

His abfent beams, had lighted up the fky;

When Philomel, officious all the day

To fing the fervice of th' enfuing May,

Fled from her laurel fhade, and wing'd her flight,

Directly to the queen array'd in white:

And

And hopping fat familiar on her hand,
A new mufician, and increas'd the band.

The goldfinch, who, to fhun the fcalding heat,
Had chang'd the medlar for a fafer feat,
And hid in bufhes 'fcap'd the bitter fhower,
Now perch'd upon the lady of the flower;
And either fongfter, holding out their throats,
And folding up their wings, renew'd their notes:
As if all day, preluding to the fight,
They only had rehears'd, to fing by night.
The banquet ended, and the battle done,
They danc'd by ftar-light and the friendly moon:
And when they were to part, the laureat queen
Supply'd with fteeds the lady of the green;
Her and her train conducting on the way,
The moon to follow, and avoid the day.

This when I faw, inquifitive to know
The fecret moral of the myftique fhow,
I ftarted from my fhade, in hopes to find
Some nymph to fatisfy my longing mind:

And

And as my fair adventure fell, I found

A lady all in white, with laurel crown'd,

Who clos'd the rear, and foftly pac'd along,

Repeating to herfelf the former fong.

With due refpect my body I inclin'd,

As to fome being of fuperior kind,

And made my court according to the day,

Wifhing her queen and her a happy May.

Great thanks, my daughter, with a gracious bow

She faid; and I, who much defir'd to know

Of whence fhe was, yet fearful how to break

My mind, adventur'd humbly thus to fpeak:

Madam, might I prefume, and not offend,

So may the ftars and fhining moon attend

Your nightly fports, as you vouchfafe to tell,

What nymphs they were who mortal forms excel,

And what the knights who fought in lifted fields fo well.

To this the dame reply'd: Fair daughter, know,

That what you faw was all a fairy fhow:

And

And all thofe airy fhapes you now behold,

Were human bodies once, and cloth'd with earthly mold;

Our fouls, not yet prepar'd for upper light,

'Till doomfday wander in the fhades of night;

This only holiday of all the year,

We privileg'd in fun-fhine may appear:

With fongs and dance we celebrate the day,

And with due honours ufher in the May.

At other times we reign by night alone,

And pofting thro' the fkies purfue the moon:

But when the morn arifes, none are found;

For cruel Demogorgon walks the round,

And if he finds a fairy lag in light,

He drives the wretch before, and lafhes into night.

    All courteous are by kind; and ever proud,

With friendly offices to help the good.

In every land we have a larger fpace

Than what is known to you of mortal race:

Where we with green adorn our fairy bowers,

And even this grove, unfeen before, is ours.

Know

Know farther; every lady cloth'd in white,

And, crown'd with oak and laurel every knight,

Are fervants to the leaf, by liveries known

Of innocence; and I myfelf am one.

Saw you not her fo graceful to behold

In white attire, and crown'd with radiant gold?

The fovereign lady of our land is fhe,

Diana call'd, the Queen of chaftity:

And, for the fpotlefs name of maid fhe bears,

That Agnus-caftus in her hand appears;

And all her train, with leafy chaplets crown'd,

Were for unblam'd virginity renown'd;

But thofe the chief, and higheft in command,

Who bear thofe holy branches in their hand:

The knights, adorn'd with laurel crowns, are they

Whom death nor danger ever could difmay,

Victorious names, who made the world obey:

Who, while they liv'd, in deeds of arms excell'd,

And after death for deities were held.

But

But thofe, who wear the woodbine on their brow, :
Were knights of love, who never broke their vow;
Firm to their plighted faith, and ever free
From fears and fickle chance, and jealoufy:
The lords and ladies who the woodbine bear,
As true as Triftram and Ifotta were.

But what are thofe, faid I, th' unconquer'd nine,
Who crown'd with laurel-wreaths in golden armour
    fhine ?
And who the knights in green, and what the train
Of ladies drefs'd with daifies on the plain?
Why both the bands in worfhip difagree,
And fome adore the flower, and fome the tree?

Juft is your fuit, fair daughter, faid the dame:
Thofe laurell'd chiefs were men of mighty fame;
Nine worthies were they call'd, of different rites,
Three jews, three pagans, and three chriftian knights.
Thefe, as you fee, ride foremoft in the field,
As they the foremoft rank of honour held,
And all in deeds of chivalry excell'd:

                             Their

Their temples wreath'd with leaves, that ſtill renew;

For deathleſs laurel is the victor's due:

Who bear the bows were knights in Arthur's reign,

Twelve they, and twelve the peers of Charlemain:

For bows the ſtrength of brawny arms imply,

Emblems of valour, and of victory.

Behold an order yet of newer date,

Doubling their number, equal in their ſtate:

Our England's ornament, the crown's defence,

·In battle brave, protectors of their prince:

Unchang'd by fortune, to their ſovereign true,

For which their manly legs are bound with blue.

Theſe, of the garter call'd, of faith unſtain'd,

In fighting fields the laurel have obtain'd,

And well repaid the honours which they gain'd.

The laurel wreaths were firſt by Cæſar worn;

And ſtill they Cæſar's ſucceſſors adorn:

One leaf of this is immortality,

And more of worth than all the world can buy.

One doubt remains, faid I: the dames in green,

What were their qualities, and who their queen?

Flora commands, faid fhe, thofe nymphs and knights,

Who liv'd in flothful eafe and loofe delights;

Who never acts of honour durft purfue,

The men inglorious knights, the ladies all untrue:

Who nurs'd in idlenefs, and train'd in courts,

Pafs'd all their precious hours in plays and fports,

'Till death behind came ftalking on, unfeen,

And wither'd (like the ftorm) the frefhnefs of their green.

Thefe, and their mates, enjoy their prefent hour,

And therefore pay their homage to the flower.

But knights in knightly deeds fhould perfevere,

And ftill continue what at firft they were;

Continue, and proceed in honour's fair carreer.

No room for cowardice, or dull delay;

From good to better they fhould urge their way.

For this with golden fpurs the chiefs are grac'd,

With pointed rowels arm'd, to mend their hafte;

For

For this with lafting leaves their brows are bound;
For laurel is the fign of labour crown'd,
Which bears the bitter blaft, nor fhaken falls to ground:
From winter winds it fuffers no decay,
For ever frefh and fair, and every month is May:
Ev'n when the vital fap retreats below,
Ev'n when the hoary head is hid in fnow;
The life is in the leaf, and ftill between
The fits of falling fnow appears the ftreaky green.
Not fo the flower; which lafts for little fpace,
A fhort-liv'd good, and an uncertain grace;
This way and that the feeble ftem is driven,
Weak to fuftain the ftorms, and injuries of heaven.
Propp'd by the fpring it lifts aloft the head,
But of a fickly beauty, foon to fhed;
In fummer living, and in winter dead.
For things of tender kind, for pleafure made,
Shoot up with fwift increafe, and fudden are decay'd.

With

With humble words, the wifeſt I could frame,

And proffer'd ſervice, I repaid the dame;

That, of her grace, ſhe gave her maid to know

The ſecret meaning of this moral ſhow.

And ſhe, to prove what profit I had made

Of myſtic truth, in fables firſt convey'd,

Demanded, till the next returning May,

Whether the leaf or flower I would obey?

I choſe the leaf; ſhe ſmil'd with ſober chear,

And wiſh'd me fair adventure for the year;

And gave me charms and ſigils, for defence

Againſt ill tongues, that ſcandal innocence:

But I, ſaid ſhe, my fellows muſt purſue,

Already paſt the plain, and out of view.

  We parted thus; I homeward ſped my way,

Bewilder'd in the wood till dawn of day:

And met the merry crew who danc'd about the May.

Then late, refreſh'd with ſleep, I roſe to write

The viſionary vigils of the night:

Bluſh,

Blufh, as thou may'ft, my little book, with fhame,

Nor hope with homely verfe to purchafe fame;

For fuch thy Maker chofe; and fo defign'd

Thy fimple ftile to fuit thy lowly kind.

ODE

ODE ON ST. CECILIA'S DAY.

BY THE SAME.

I.

'Twas at the royal feaſt, for Perſia won,

By Philip's warlike ſon:

Aloft in awful ſtate

The godlike hero ſat

On his imperial throne:

His valiant peers were plac'd around;

Their brows with roſes and with myrtles bound;

(So ſhould deſert in arms be crown'd:)

The lovely Thais, by his ſide,

Sat like a blooming Eaſtern bride,

In flower of youth and beauty's pride.

Happy, happy, happy pair!

None but the brave,

None but the brave,

None but the brave deſerves the fair.

CHORUS.

CHORUS.

Happy, happy, happy pair!
None but the brave,
None but the brave,
None but the brave deferves the fair.

II.

Timotheus, plac'd on high
  Amid the tuneful quire,
    With flying fingers touch'd the lyre:
The trembling notes afcend the fky,
             And heavenly joys infpire.

The fong began from Jove,
Who left his blifsful feats above,
(Such is the power of mighty love)
A dragon's fiery form bely'd the god:
Sublime on radiant fpires he rode,
    When he to fair Olympia prefs'd;
    And while he fought her fnowy breaft:
Then, round her flender waift he curl'd,
Andftamp'danimageofhimfelf,afovereignoftheworld.

      K   The

The liftening crowd admire the lofty found

A prefent deity, they fhout around:

A prefent deity, the vaulted roofs rebound:

   With ravifh'd ears

   The monarch hears,

   Affumes the god,

   Affects to nod,

  And feems to fhake the fpheres.

C H O R U S.

   With ravifh'd ears

   The monarch hears,

   Affumes the god,

   Affects to nod,

  And feems to fhake the fpheres.

III.

The praife of Bacchus then, the fweet mufician fung;

  Of Bacchus, ever fair and ever young:

   The jolly god in triumph comes;

   Sound the trumpets; beat the drums;

          Flufh'd

Flush'd with a purple grace

He shews his honest face.

Now give the hautboys breath; he comes, he comes.

Bacchus, ever fair and young,

Drinking joys did first ordain;

Bacchus' blessings are a treasure,

Drinking is the soldier's pleasure;

Rich the treasure,

Sweet the pleasure,

Sweet is pleasure after pain.

C H O R U S.

Bacchus' blessings are a treasure,

Drinking is the soldier's pleasure;

Rich the treasure,

Sweet the pleasure,

Sweet is pleasure after pain.

IV.

Sooth'd with the sound, the king grew vain;

Fought all his battles o'er again;

And thrice he routed all his foes; and thrice he slew

the slain.

K 2 The

The mafter faw the madnefs rife ;

His glowing cheeks, his ardent eyes ;

And while he heaven and earth defy'd,

Chang'd his hand, and check'd his pride.

He chofe a mournful mufe

Soft pity to infufe :

He fung Darius great and good,

By too fevere a fate,

Fallen, fallen, fallen, fallen,

Fallen from his high eftate,

And weltering in his blood ;

Deferted, at his utmoft need,

By thofe his former bounty fed :

On the bare earth expos'd he lies,

With not a friend to clofe his eyes.

With down-caft looks the joylefs victor fat,

Revolving in his alter'd foul

The various turns of chance below ;

And, now and then, a figh he ftole ;

And tears began to flow.

CHORUS.

C H O R U S.

Revolving in his alter'd foul
  The various turns of chance below;
And, now and then, a figh he ftole;
  And tears began to flow.

V.

The mighty mafter fmil'd, to fee
That love was in the next degree:
'Twas but a kindred-found to move,
For pity melts the mind to love.

  Softly fweet, in Lydian meafures,
  Soon he footh'd his foul to pleafures.
War, he fung, is toil and trouble;
Honour but an empty bubble;
  Never ending, ftill beginning,
Fighting ftill, and ftill deftroying:
  If the world be worth thy winning,
Think, O think, it worth enjoying:
  Lovely Thais fits befide thee,
  Take the good the gods provide thee.

The

The many rend the ſkies with loud applauſe;

So Love was crown'd, but Muſic won the cauſe.

The prince, unable to conceal his pain,

Gaz'd on the fair

Who caus'd his care,

And ſigh'd and look'd, ſigh'd and look'd,

Sigh'd and look'd, and ſigh'd again:

At length, with love and wine at once oppreſs'd,

The vanquiſh'd victor ſunk upon her breaſt.

C H O R U S.

The prince, unable to conceal his pain,

Gaz'd on the fair

Who caus'd his care,

And ſigh'd and look'd, ſigh'd and look'd,

Sigh'd and look'd, and ſigh'd again:

At length, with love and wine at once oppreſs'd,

The vanquiſh'd victor ſunk upon her breaſt.

VI. Now

VI.

Now ſtrike the golden lyre again :

A louder yet, and yet a louder ſtrain.

Break his bands of ſleep aſunder,

And rouſe him like a rattling peal of thunder.

Hark, hark ! the horrid ſound

Has rais'd up his head :

As awak'd from the dead,

And amaz'd, he ſtares around.

Revenge, revenge ! Timotheus cries,

See the furies ariſe :

See the ſnakes that they rear,

How they hiſs in their hair,

And the ſparkles that flaſh from their eyes !

Behold a ghaſtly band,

Each a torch in his hand !

Thoſe are Grecian ghoſts, that in battle were ſlain,

And unbury'd remain

Inglorious on the plain :

Give the vengeance due

To the valiant crew :

K 4   Behold

Behold how they toſs their torches on high,

How they point to the Perſian abodes,

And glittering temples of their hoſtile gods.

The princes applaud with a furious joy;

'And the king ſeiz'd a flambeau with zeal to deſtroy;

Thais led the way,

To light him to his prey,

And, like another Helen, fir'd another Troy.

C H O R U S.

And the king ſeiz'd a flambeau with zeal to deſtroy;

Thais led the way,

To light him to his prey,

And, like another Helen, fir'd another Troy.

VII.

Thus, long ago,

Ere heaving bellows learn'd to blow,

While organs yet were mute;

Timotheus, to his breathing flute,

And

And founding lyre,

Could fwell the foul to rage, or kindle foft defire.

At laft divine Cecilia came,

Inventrefs of the vocal frame;

The fweet enthufiaft, from her facred ftore,

Enlarg'd the former narrow bounds,

And added length to folemn founds,

With nature's mother-wit, and arts unknown before.

Let old Timotheus yield the prize,

Or both divide the crown;

He rais'd a mortal to the fkies;

She drew an angel down.

GRAND CHORUS.

At laft divine Cecilia came,

Inventrefs of the vocal frame;

The fweet enthufiaft, from her facred ftore,

Enlarg'd the former narrow bounds,

And added length to folemn founds,

With nature's mother-wit, and arts unknown before.

Let

Let old Timotheus yield the prize,

   Or both divide the crown;

He rais'd a mortal to the ſkies;

   She drew an angel down.

L' ALLEGRO.

L' ALLEGRO.

BY MILTON.

HENCE, loathed Melancholy,

Of Cerberus, and blackeſt Midnight born,

In Stygian cave forlorn,

'Mongſt horrid ſhapes, and ſhrieks, and fights unholy,

Find out ſome uncouth cell,

   Where brooding Darkneſs ſpreads his jealous wings,

And the night-raven ſings;

   There under ebon ſhades, and low-brow'd rocks,

   As ragged as thy locks,

In dark Cimmerian deſert ever dwell.

But come, thou Goddeſs fair and free,

In heaven yclep'd Euphroſyne,

And by men, heart-eaſing Mirth,

Whom lovely Venus at a birth

With two ſiſter Graces more

To ivy-crowned Bacchus bore;

                              Or

Or whether (as fome fages fing)
The frolic wind that breathes the fpring,
Zephyr, with Aurora playing,
As he met her once a Maying,
There on beds of violets blue,
And frefh-blown rofes wafh'd in dew,
Fill'd her with thee a daughter fair,
So buxom, blithe, and debonair.

    Hafte thee, Nymph, and bring with thee
Jeft and youthful Jollity,
Quips and Cranks, and wanton Wiles,
Nods and Becks, and wreathed Smiles,
Such as hang on Hebe's cheek, ·
And love to live in dimple fleek ;
Sport that wrinkled Care derides,
And Laughter holding both his fides ;
Come, and trip it as you go
On the light fantaftic toe,
And in thy right hand lead with thee
The mountain nymph, fweet Liberty ;

                             And,

And, if I give thee honour due,

Mirth, admit me of thy crew,

To live with her, and live with thee,

In unreproved pleafures free;

To hear the lark begin his flight,

And finging ftartle the dull night,

From his watch-tower in the fkies,

'Till the dappled dawn doth rife;

Then to come, in fpite of forrow,

And at my window bid good-morrow,

Through the fweet-briar, or the vine,

Or the twifted eglantine:

While the cock with lively din

Scatters the rear of darknefs thin,

And to the ftack, or the barn-door,

Stoutly ftruts his dames before:

Oft liftening, how the hounds and horn

Chearly roufe the flumbering morn,

From the fide of fome hoar hill,

Through the high wood echoing fhrill:

Some

Some time walking not unſeen
By hedge-row elms, on hillocks green,
Right againſt the eaſtern gate,
Where the great ſun begins his ſtate,
Rob'd in flames and amber light,
The clouds in thouſand liveries dight,
While the plough-man near at hand
Whiſtles o'er the furrow'd land,
And the milk-maid ſingeth blithe,
And the mower whets his ſcythe,
And every ſhepherd tells his tale
Under the hawthorn in the dale.

Straight mine eye hath caught new pleaſures,
Whilſt the landſkip round it meaſures,
Ruſſet lawns, and fallows gray,
Where the nibbling flocks do ſtray,
Mountains on whoſe barren breaſt
The labouring clouds do often reſt,
Meadows trim with daiſies pied,
Shallow brooks, and rivers wide.

Towers

Towers and battlements it fees

Bofom'd high in tufted trees,

Where perhaps fome beauty lies,

The Cynofure of neighbouring eyes:

Hard by, a cottage chimney fmokes,

From betwixt two aged oaks,

Where Corydon and Thyrfis met,

Are at their favoury dinner fet

Of herbs, and other country meffes,

Which the neat-handed Phyllis dreffes;

And then in hafte her bower fhe leaves,

With Theftylis to bind the fheaves;

Or, if the earlier feafon lead,

To the tann'd hay-cock in the mead.

Sometimes with fecure delight

The upland hamlets will invite,

When the merry bells ring round,

And the jocund rebecks found

To many a youth, and many a maid,

Dancing in the chequer'd fhade;

And

And young and old come forth to play

On a funſhine holiday,

Till the live-long day-light fail;

Then to the ſpicy nut-brown ale,

With ſtories told of many a feat,

How fairy Mab the junkets eat;

She was pinch'd, and pull'd, ſhe ſaid,

And he, by friar's lanthorn led,

Tells how the drudging Goblin ſweat

To earn his cream-bowl duly ſet,

When in one night, ere glimpſe of morn,

His ſhadowy flail hath threſh'd the corn,

That ten day-labourers could not end;

Then lies him down the lubbar fiend,

And ſtretch'd out all the chimney's length,

Baſks at the fire his hairy ſtrength,

And cropful out of doors he flings,

Ere the firſt cock his mattin rings.

Thus done the tales, to bed they creep,

By whiſpering winds ſoon lull'd aſleep.

Towered

Towered cities pleafe us then,
And the bufy hum of men,   ·
Where throngs of knights and barons bold
In weeds of peace high triumphs hold;
With ftore of ladies, whofe bright eyes
Rain influence, and judge the prize
Of wit, or arms, while both contend
To win her grace, whom all commend.
There let Hymen oft appear
In faffron robe, with taper clear,
And pomp, and feaft, and revelry,
With mafk and antique pageantry;
Such fights as youthful poets dream,
On fummer eves by haunted ftream.
Then to the well-trod ftage anon,
If Jonfon's learned fock be on,
Or fweeteft Shakefpeare, Fancy's child,
Warble his native wood-notes wild.

And ever againft eating cares
Lap me in foft Lydian airs;

L   Married

Married to immortal verfe,

Such as the meeting foul may pierce,

In notes, with many a winding bout

Of linked fweetnefs long drawn out,

With wanton heed, and giddy cunning,

The melting voice through mazes running,

Untwifting all the chains that tie

The hidden foul of Harmony;

That Orpheus' felf may heave his head

From golden flumber, on a bed

Of heapt Elyfian flowers, and hear

Such ftrains as would have won the ear

Of Pluto, to have quite fet free

His half-regain'd Eurydice.

    Thefe delights if thou canft give,

Mirth, with thee I mean to live.

IL PENSEROSO.

BY THE SAME.

H ᴇ ɴ ᴄ ᴇ, vain deluding joys,

    The brood of Folly, without father bred!

How little you befted,

    Or fill the fixed mind with all your toys!

Dwell in fome idle brain,

And fancies fond with gaudy fhapes poffefs,

As thick and numberlefs

    As the gay motes that people the fun-beams,

Or likeft hovering dreams,

    The fickle penfioners of Morpheus' train.

    But hail, thou Goddefs, fage and holy!

Hail, divineft Melancholy!

Whofe faintly vifage is too bright

To hit the fenfe of human fight,

And therefore to our weaker view,

O'erlaid with black, ftaid Wifdom's hue;

        Black,

Black, but fuch as in efteem
Prince Memnon's fifter might befeem,
Or that ftarr'd Ethiop queen that ftrove
To fet her beauty's praife above
The fea-nymphs, and their powers offended:
Yet thou art higher far defcended;
Thee bright hair'd Vefta, long of yore,
To folitary Saturn bore;
His daughter fhe (in Saturn's reign
Such mixture was not held a ftain)
Oft in glimmering bowers and glades
He met her, and in fecret fhades
Of woody Ida's inmoft grove,
While yet there was no fear of Jove.

 Come, penfive Nun, devout and pure,
. Sober, ftedfaft, and demure,
All in a robe of darkeft grain,
Flowing with majeftic train,
And fable ftole of Cyprus lawn,
Over thy decent fhoulders drawn:

Come,

Come, but keep thy wonted ſtate,

With even ſtep, and muſing gait,

And looks commercing with the ſkies,

Thy rapt ſoul ſitting in thine eyes;

There, held in holy paſſion ſtill,

Forget thyſelf to marble, till

With a ſad leaden downward caſt

Thou fix them on the earth as faſt:

And join with thee calm Peace, and Quiet,

Spare Faſt, that oft with Gods doth diet,

And hears the Muſes in a ring

Aye round about Jove's altar ſing;

And add to theſe retired Leiſure,

That in trim gardens takes his pleaſure:

But firſt, and chiefeſt, with thee bring

Him that yon ſoars on golden wing,

Guiding the fiery wheeled throne,

The Cherub Contemplation:

And the mute Silence hiſt along,

'Leſs Philomel will deign a ſong,

In

In her fweeteft, faddeft plight,

Smoothing the rugged brow of night,

While Cynthia checks her dragon yoke,

Gently o'er the accuftom'd oak ;

Sweet bird, that fhunn'ft the noife of folly,

Moft mufical, moft melancholy !

Thee, chauntrefs, oft, the woods among,

I woo to hear thy even-fong :

And miffing thee, I walk unfeen

On the dry fmooth-fhaven green,

To behold the wandering moon,

Riding near her higheft noon,

Like one that had been led aftray

Through the heaven's wide pathlefs way ;

And oft, as if her head fhe bow'd,

Stooping through a fleecy cloud.

　　Oft on a plat of rifing ground,

I hear the far-off Curfew found,

Over fome wide-water'd fhore,

Swinging flow with fullen roar.

　　　　　　　　　　　　Or

Or if the air will not permit,

Some ſtill removed place will fit,

Where glowing embers through the room

Teach light to counterfeit a gloom;

Far from all reſort of mirth,

Save the cricket on the hearth,

Or the bellman's drowſy charm,

To bleſs the doors from nightly harm.

Or let my lamp at midnight hour

Be ſeen in ſome high lonely tower;

Where I may oft out-watch the Bear,

With thrice great Hermes, or unſphere

The ſpirit of Plato, to unfold

What worlds, or what vaſt regions, hold

The immortal mind that hath forſook

Her manſion in this fleſhly nook:

And of thoſe dæmons that are found

In fire, air, flood, or under ground,

Whoſe power hath a true conſent

With planet, or with element.

Sometime

Sometime let gorgeous Tragedy

In fcepter'd pall come fweeping by,

Prefenting Thebes', or Pelops' line,

Or the tale of Troy divine,

Or what (though rare) of later age,

Ennobled hath the bufkin'd ftage.

But, O fad Virgin, that thy power

Might raife Mufæus from his bower,

Or bid the foul of Orpheus fing

Such notes as, warbled to the ftring,

Drew iron tears down Pluto's cheek,

And made hell grant what love did feek :

Or call up him that left half-told

The ftory of Cambufcan bold,

Of Camball, and of Algarfife,

And who had Canacé to wife,

That own'd the virtuous ring and glafs,

And of the wonderous horfe of brafs,

On which the Tartar king did ride ;

And if aught elfe great bards befide

In

In fage and folemn tunes have fung,

Of tourneys and of trophies hung,

Of forefts, and enchantments drear,

Where more is meant than meets the ear.

Thus night oft fee me in thy pale career,

Till civil-fuited morn appear,

Not trick'd and frounc'd as fhe was wont

With the Attic boy to hunt,

But kerchief'd in a comely cloud,

While rocking winds are piping loud,

Or ufher'd with a fhower ftill,

When the guft hath blown his fill,

Ending on the ruftling leaves,

With minute drops from off the eaves.

And when the fun begins to fling

His flaring beams, me, Goddefs, bring

To arched walks of twilight groves,

And fhadows brown that Sylvan loves

Of pine, or monumental oak,

Where the rude ax with heaved ftroke

Was

Was never heard the Nymphs to daunt,,

Or fright them from their hallow'd haunt.

There in clofe covert by fome brook,

Where no profaner eye may look,

Hide me from day's garifh eye,

While the bee with honeyed thigh,

That at her flowery work doth fing,

And the waters murmuring,

With fuch concert as they keep,

Entice the dewy-feather'd fleep:

And let fome ftrange myfterious dream,

Wave at his wings in airy ftream

Of lively portraiture difplay'd,

Softly on my eye-lids laid;

And as I wake, fweet mufic breathe

Above, about, or underneath,

Sent by fome fpirit to mortals good,

Or the unfeen Genius of the wood.

But let my due feet never fail

To walk the ftudious cloyfter's pale,

And

And love the high embowed roof,

With antique pillars maffy proof,

And ftoried windows richly dight,

Cafting a dim religious light.

There let the pealing organ blow,

To the full-voic'd quire below,

In fervice high, and anthems clear,

As may with fweetnefs, through mine ear,

Diffolve me into extafies,

And bring all heaven before mine eyes.

   And may at laft my weary age

Find out the peaceful hermitage,

The hairy gown and moffy cell,

Where I may fit, and rightly fpell

Of every ftar that heaven doth fhew,

And every herb that fips the dew;

'Till old experience do attain

To fomething like prophetic ftrain.

   Thefe pleafures, Melancholy, give,

And I with thee will choofe to live.

DIRGE

DIRGE IN CYMBELINE.

BY MR. W. COLLINS.

To fair FIDELE's graffy tomb
    Soft maids and village hinds fhall brin⌐
Each opening fweet, of earlieft bloom,
    And rifle all the breathing Spring.

No wailing ghoft fhall dare appear
    To vex with fhrieks this quiet grove,
But fhepherd lads affemble here,
    And melting virgins own their love.

No wither'd witch fhall here be feen,
    No goblins lead their nightly crew;
The female fays fhall haunt the green,
    And drefs thy grave with pearly dew.

                        The

The red-breaſt oft, at evening hours,
   Shall kindly lend his little aid,
With hoary moſs, and gather'd flowers,
   To deck the ground where thou art laid.

When howling winds, and beating rain,
   In tempeſts ſhake thy ſylvan cell,
Or 'midſt the chace on every plain,
   The tender thought on thee ſhall dwell;

Each lonely ſcene ſhall thee reſtore,
   For thee the tear be duly ſhed;
Belov'd, till life can charm no more;
   And mourn'd, till Pity's ſelf be dead.

ODE

ODE

ON THE PROSPECT OF ETON COLLEGE.

BY MR. GRAY.

Y E diftant fpires, ye antique towers,
That crown the watery glade,
Where grateful Science ftill adores
Her HENRY's * holy Shade;
And ye, that from the ftately brow
Of WINDSOR's heights the expanfe below
Of grove, of lawn, of mead furvey,
Whofe turf, whofe fhade, whofe flowers among
Wanders the hoary Thames along
His filver-winding way.

---

* King HENRY the Sixth, Founder of the College.

Ah

Ah happy hills, ah pleaſing ſhade,

Ah fields belov'd in vain,

Where once my careleſs childhood ſtray'd,

A ſtranger yet to pain !

I feel the gales, that from ye blow,

A momentary bliſs beſtow,

As waving freſh their gladſome wing,

My weary ſoul they ſeem to ſooth,

And, redolent of joy and youth,

To breathe a ſecond ſpring.

Say, Father THAMES, for thou haſt ſeen

Full many a ſprightly race

Diſporting on thy margent green

The paths of pleaſure trace,

Who foremoſt now delight to cleave

With pliant arm thy glaſſy wave?

The captive linnet which enthrall?

What idle progeny ſucceed

To chaſe the rolling circle's ſpeed,

Or urge the flying ball?

While

While fome, on earneft bufinefs bent,

Their murmuring labours ply

'Gainft graver hours, that bring conftraint

To fweeten liberty :

Some bold adventurers difdain

The limits of their little reign,

And unknown regions dare defcry :

Still as they run they look behind,

They hear a voice in every wind,

And fnatch a fearful joy.

Gay hope is theirs, by fancy fed,

Lefs pleafing when poffeft ;

The tear forgot as foon as fhed,

The funfhine of the breaft :

Theirs buxom health of rofy hue,

Wild wit, invention ever new,

And lively chear of vigour born ;

The thoughtlefs day, the eafy night,

The fpirits pure, the flumbers light,

That fly the approach of morn.

Alas,

Alas, regardlefs of their doom,

The little victims play!

No fenfe have they of ills to come,

Nor care beyond to-day:

Yet fee, how all around them wait

The minifters of human fate,

And black Misfortune's baleful train!

Ah, fhew them where in ambufh ftand,

To feize their prey, the murderous band!

Ah, tell them they are men!

Thefe fhall the fury Paffions tear,

The vultures of the mind,

Difdainful Anger, pallid Fear,

And Shame, that fkulks behind;

Or pining Love fhall wafte their youth,

Or Jealoufy, with rankling tooth,

That inly gnaws the fecret heart;

And Envy wan, and faded Care,

Grim-vifag'd comfortlefs Defpair,

And Sorrow's piercing dart.

M   Ambition

Ambition this ſhall tempt to riſe,

Then whirl the wretch from high,

To bitter Scorn a ſacrifice,

And grinning Infamy :

The ſtings of Falſehood thoſe ſhall try,

And hard Unkindneſs' alter'd eye,

That mocks the tear it forc'd to flow;

And keen Remorſe with blood defil'd,

And moody Madneſs laughing wild

Amid ſevereſt woe.

Lo ! in the vale of years beneath

A griſly troop are ſeen,

The painful family of Death,

More hideous than their Queen :

This racks the joints, this fires the veins,

That every labouring finew ſtrains,

Thoſe in the deeper vitals rage :

Lo! Poverty, to fill the band,

That numbs the ſoul with icy hand,

And ſlow-conſuming Age.

To

To each his fufferings: all are men,
Condemn'd alike to groan;
The tender for another's pain,
The unfeeling for his own.
Yet, ah! why fhould they know their fate?
Since forrow never comes too late,
And happinefs too fwiftly flies:
Thought would deftroy their paradife;
No more—where ignorance is blifs,
'Tis folly to be wife.

HYMN

HYMN TO ADVERSITY.

BY THE SAME.

Daughter of Jove, relentlefs Power,
Thou tamer of the human breaft,
Whofe iron fcourge, and torturing hour,
The bad affright, afflict the beft!
Bound in thy adamantine chain,
The proud are taught to tafte of pain,
And purple tyrants vainly groan
With pangs unfelt before, unpitied and alone.

When firft thy Sire to fend on earth
Virtue, his darling child, defign'd,
To thee he gave the heavenly birth,
And bade to form her infant mind.
Stern rugged nurfe! thy rigid lore
With patience many a year fhe bore:
What forrow was, thou bad'ft her know,
And from her own fhe learnt to melt at others' woe.

Scar'd

Scar'd at thy frown terrific, fly

Self-pleafing Folly's idle brood,

Wild Laughter, Noife, and thoughtlefs Joy,

And leave us leifure to be good.

Light they difperfe; and with them go

The fummer-friend, the flattering foe;

By vain Profperity receiv'd,

To her they vow their truth, and are again believ'd.

Wifdom in fable garb array'd,

Immers'd in rapturous thought profound,

And Melancholy, filent maid

With leaden eye, that loves the ground,

Still on thy folemn fteps attend:

Warm Charity, the general friend,

With Juftice, to herfelf fevere,

And Pity, dropping foft the fadly-pleafing tear.

Oh, gently on thy fuppliant's head,

Dread Goddefs, lay thy chaftening hand!

M 3

Not

Not in thy Gorgon terrors clad,

Nor circled with the vengeful band

(As by the impious thou art feen)

With thundering voice, and threatening mien,

With fcreaming Horror's funeral cry,

Defpair, and fell Difeafe, and ghaftly Poverty.

Thy form benign, Oh Goddefs, wear,

Thy milder influence impart;

Thy philofophic train be there

To foften, not to wound my heart:

The generous fpark extinct revive,

Teach me to love and to forgive,

Exact my own defects to fcan,

What others are to feel; and know myfelf a man.

ODE

ODE ON THE SPRING.

BY THE SAME.

Lo! where the rofy-bofom'd Hours,
Fair VENUS' train appear,
Difclofe the long-expecting flowers,
And wake the purple year!
The Attic warbler pours her throat,
Refponfive to the cuckow's note,
The untaught harmony of fpring:
While, whifpering pleafure as they fly,
Cool Zephyrs thro' the clear blue fky
Their gather'd fragrance fling.

Where'er the oak's thick branches ftretch
A broader browner fhade;
Where'er the rude and mofs-grown beech
O'er-canopies the glade,

Befide

Befide fome water's rufhy brink
With me the Mufe fhall fit, and think
(At eafe reclin'd in ruftic ftate)
How vain the ardour of the Crowd,
How low, how little are the Proud,
How indigent the Great!

    Still is the toiling hand of Care:
The panting herds repofe:
Yet hark, how thro' the peopled air
The bufy murmur glows!
The infect youth are on the wing,
Eager to tafte the honied fpring,
And float amid the liquid noon:
Some lightly o'er the current fkim,
Some fhew their gayly-gilded trim
Quick-glancing to the fun.

To

To Contemplation's sober eye '
Such is the race of Man:
And they that creep, and they that fly,
Shall end where they began.
Alike the Busy and the Gay
But flutter thro' life's little day,
In fortune's varying colours drest:
Brush'd by the hand of rough Mischance,
Or chill'd by age, their airy dance
They leave, in dust to rest.

Methinks I hear in accents low
The sportive kind reply:
Poor moralist! and what art thou?
A solitary fly!
Thy joys no glittering female meets,
No hive hast thou of hoarded sweets,
No painted plumage to display:
On hasty wings thy youth is flown;
Thy sun is set, thy spring is gone——
We frolic, while 'tis May.

ODE

ODE ON THE PROGRESS OF POESY.

BY THE SAME.

I. 1.

Awake, Æolian lyre, awake,
And give to rapture all thy trembling ftrings.
From Helicon's harmonious fprings
A thoufand rills their mazy progrefs take:
The laughing flowers, that round them blow,
Drink life and fragrance as they flow.
Now the rich ftream of mufic winds along,
Deep, majeftic, fmooth, and ftrong,
Thro' verdant vales, and Ceres' golden reign:
Now rolling down the fteep amain,
Headlong, impetuous, fee it pour:
The rocks, and nodding groves, rebellow to the roar.

I. 2. Oh

I. 2.

Oh! fovereign of the willing foul,
Parent of fweet and folemn-breathing airs,
Enchanting fhell! the fullen Cares,
And frantic Paffions, hear thy foft controul.
On Thracia's hills the Lord of War
Has curb'd the fury of his car,
And dropp'd his thirfty lance at thy command:
Perching on the fcepter'd hand
Of Jove, thy magic lulls the feather'd king
With ruffled plumes, and flagging wing:
Quench'd in dark clouds of flumber lie
The terror of his beak, and lightnings of his eye.

I. 3.

Thee the voice, the dance, obey,
Temper'd to thy warbled lay.
O'er Idalia's velvet-green
The rofy-crowned Loves are feen
On Cytherea's day

With

With antic fports, and blue-eyed Pleafures,

Frifking light in frolic meafures;

Now purfuing, now retreating,

Now in circling troops they meet:

To brifk notes in cadence beating

Glance their many-twinkling feet.

Slow melting ftrains their Queen's approach declare:

Where'er fhe turns the Graces homage pay;

With arms fublime, that float upon the air,

In gliding ftate fhe wins her eafy way:

O'er her warm cheek, and rifing bofom, move

The bloom of young Defire, and purple light of Love.

II. 1.

Man's feeble race what ills await,

Labour, and Penury, the racks of Pain,

Difeafe, and Sorrow's weeping train,

And Death, fad refuge from the ftorms of Fate!

The fond complaint, my fong, difprove,

And juftify the laws of Jove.

Say,

Say, has he given in vain the heavenly Mufe?

Night, and all her fickly dews,

Her fpectres wan, and birds of boding cry,

He gives to range the dreary fky:

'Till down the eaftern cliffs afar

Hyperion's march they fpy, and glittering fhafts of war.

II. 2.

In climes beyond the folar road,

Where fhaggy forms o'er ice-built mountains roam,

The Mufe has broke the twilight-gloom

To chear the fhivering native's dull abode:

And oft, beneath the odorous fhade

Of Chili's boundlefs forefts laid,

She deigns to hear the favage youth repeat,

In loofe numbers wildly fweet,

Their feather-cinctur'd Chiefs, and dufky Loves:

Her track, where'er the goddefs roves,

Glory purfue, and generous fhame,

The unconquerable mind, and freedom's holy flame.

II. 3. Woods,

II. 3.

Woods, that wave o'er Delphi's steep,

Isles, that crown the Ægean deep,

Fields, that cool Ilissus laves,

Or where Mæander's amber waves

In lingering labyrinths creep,

How do your tuneful Echos languish,

Mute, but to the voice of anguish !

Where each old poetic mountain

Inspiration breath'd around,

Every shade and hallow'd fountain

Murmur'd deep a solemn sound;

Till the sad Nine, in Greece's evil hour,

Left their Parnassus for the Latian plains.

Alike they scorn the pomp of tyrant-power,

And coward vice, that revels in her chains;

When Latium had her lofty spirit lost,

They sought, oh Albion ! next thy sea-encircled coast.

III. 1. Far

III. 1.

Far from the fun and fummer-gale,

In thy green lap was Nature's * Darling laid,

What time, where lucid Avon ftray'd,

To him the mighty mother did unveil

Her awful face: The dauntlefs child

Stretch'd forth his little arms, and fmil'd.

This pencil take (fhe faid) whofe colours clear

Richly paint the vernal year:

Thine too thefe golden keys, immortal boy !

This can unlock the gates of joy ;

Of horror that, and thrilling fears,

Or ope the facred fource of fympathetic tears.

III. 2.

Nor fecond he †, that rode fublime

Upon the feraph-wings of extafy,

The fecrets of the abyfs to fpy.

He pafs'd the flaming bounds of place and time:

---

* SHAKESPEARE.   † MILTON.

The

The living throne, the faphire-blaze,

Where Angels tremble, while they gaze,

He faw; but blafted with excefs of light,

Clos'd his eyes in endlefs night.

Behold, where DRYDEN's lefs prefumptuous car

Wide o'er the fields of glory bear

Two courfers of ethereal race,

With necks in thunder cloth'd, and long-refounding

    pace.

III. 3.

Hark, his hands the lyre explore !

Bright-eyed Fancy hovering o'er

Scatters from her pictur'd urn

Thoughts that breathe, and words that burn.

But ah ! 'tis heard no more—

Oh! Lyre divine, what daring Spirit

Wakes thee now? tho' he inherit

Nor the pride, nor ample pinion,

That the Theban Eagle bear

Sailing with fupreme dominion

Thro' the azure deep of air:

Yet

Yet oft before his infant eyes would run

Such forms, as glitter in the Mufe's ray

With orient hues, unborrow'd of the Sun:

Yet fhall he mount, and keep his diftant way

Beyond the limits of a vulgar fate,

Beneath the Good how far!—but far above the Great.

LYCIDAS:

L Y C I D A S:

AN ELEGY ON THE DEATH OF HIS FRIEND.

BY MILTON.

YET once more, O ye Laurels, and once more,
Ye Myrtles brown, with Ivy never fere,
I come to pluck your berries harfh and crude,
And with forc'd fingers rude
Shatter your leaves before the mellowing year.
Bitter conftraint, and fad occafion dear,
Compels me to difturb your feafon due:
For LYCIDAS is dead! dead ere his prime,
Young LYCIDAS, and hath not left his peer:
Who would not fing for LYCIDAS? he knew
Himfelf to fing, and build the lofty rhime.
He muft not float upon his watery bier
Unwept, and welter to the parching wind,
Without the meed of fome melodious tear.

Begin

Begin then, Sifters of the facred well,

That from beneath the feat of Jove doth fpring,

Begin, and fomewhat loudly fweep the ftring.

Hence with denial vain, and coy excufe,

So may fome gentle Mufe

With lucky words favour my deftin'd urn,

And as he paffes turn,

And bid fair peace be to my fable fhroud :

For we were nurft upon the felf-fame hill,

Fed the fame flock by fountain, fhade, and rill.

Together both, ere the high lawns appear'd

Under the opening eye-lids of the morn,

We drove afield, and both together heard

What time the gray-fly winds her fultry horn ;

Battening our flocks with the frefh dews of night,

Oft till the ftar, that rofe, at evening, bright,

Toward Heaven's defcent had flop'd his weftering wheel.

Mean while the rural ditties were not mute,

Temper'd to the oaten flute,

Rough Satyrs danc'd, and Fauns with cloven heel

From

From the glad found would not be abfent long,
And old Damætas lov'd to hear our fong.

But Oh the heavy change, now thou art gone,
Now thou art gone, and never muft return!
Thee, Shepherd, thee the woods, and defart caves
With wild thyme and the gadding vine o'ergrown,
And all their echoes mourn.
The willows, and the hazel copfes green,
Shall now no more be feen,
Fanning their joyous leaves to thy foft lays.
As killing as the canker to the rofe,
Or taint-worm to the weanling herds that graze,
Or froft to flowers, that their gay wardrobe wear,
When firft the white-thorn blows;
Such, LYCIDAS, thy lofs to fhepherds' ear.

Where were ye, Nymphs, when the remorfelefs deep
Clos'd o'er the head of your lov'd LYCIDAS?
For neither were ye playing on the fteep,
Where your old Bards, the famous Druids, lie,
Nor on the fhaggy top of Mona high,

Nor

Nor yet where Deva fpreads her wizard ftream :

Ay me ! I fondly dream

Had ye been there, for what could that have done?

What could the Mufe herfelf that Orpheus bore,

The Mufe herfelf for her enchanting fon,

Whom univerfal nature did lament,

When, by the rout that made the hideous roar,

His goary vifage down the ftream was fent,

Down the fwift Hebrus to the Lefbian fhore?

   Alas ! what boots it with inceffant care

To tend the homely flighted fhepherd's trade,

And ftrictly meditate the thanklefs Mufe?

Were it not better done, as others ufe,

To fport with Amaryllis in the fhade,

Or with the tangles of Neæra's hair?

Fame is the fpur that the clear fpirit doth raife

(That laft infirmity of noble mind)

To fcorn delights, and live laborious days;

But the fair guerdon when we hope to find,

And

And think to burſt out into ſudden blaze,

Comes the blind Fury with the abhorred ſhears,

And ſlits the thin-ſpun life. " But not the praiſe,"

Phœbus reply'd, and touch'd my trembling ears;

" Fame is no plant that grows on mortal ſoil,

Nor in the gliſtering ſoil

Set off to the world, nor in broad rumour lies,

But lives and ſpreads aloft by thoſe pure eyes,

And perfeêt witneſs of all-judging Jove;

As he pronounces laſtly on each deed,

Of ſo much fame in Heaven expeêt thy meed."

   O fountain Arethuſe, and thou honour'd flood,

Smooth-ſliding Mincius, crown'd with vocal reeds,

That ſtrain I heard was of a higher mood:

But now my oat proceeds,

And liſtens to the herald of the ſea

That came in Neptune's plea;

He aſk'd the waves, and aſk'd the felon winds,

What hard miſhap hath doom'd this gentle ſwain?

And

And queftion'd every guft of rugged winds
That blows from off each beaked promontory;
They knew not of his ftory;
And fage Hippotades their anfwer brings,
That not a blaft was from his dungeon ftray'd,
The air was calm, and on the level brine
Sleek Panope with all her fifters play'd.
It was that fatal and perfidious bark,
Built in the eclipfe, and rigg'd with curfes dark,
That funk fo low that facred head of thine.

   Next Camus, reverend fire, went footing flow,
His mantle hairy, and his bonnet fedge,
Inwrought with figures dim, and on the edge
Like to that fanguine flower infcrib'd with woe.
Ah! who hath reft (quoth he) my deareft pledge?
Laft came, and laft did go,
The pilot of the Galilean lake,
Two maffy keys he bore, of metals twain,
(The golden opes, the iron fhuts amain)

He

He fhook his mitred locks, and ftern befpake,

" How well could I have fpar'd for thee, young fwain,

Enow of fuch as for their bellies' fake

Creep, and intrude, and climb into the fold?

Of other care they little reckoning make,

Than how to fcramble at the fhearer's feaft,

And fhove away the worthy bidden gueft;

Blind mouths! that fcarce themfelves know how to hold

A fheep-hook, or have learn'd ought elfe the leaft

That to the faithful herdman's art belongs!

What recks it them? What need they? They are fped;

And when they lift, their lean and flafhy fongs

Grate on their fcrannel pipes of wretched ftraw;

The hungry fheep look up, and are not fed,

But fwoln with wind, and the rank mift they draw,

Rot inwardly, and foul contagion fpread:

Befides what the grim wolf with privy paw

Daily devours apace, and nothing faid,

But that two-handed engine at the door

Stands ready to fmite once, and fmite no more."

Return,

Return, Alpheus, the dread voice is paſt,

That ſhrunk thy ſtreams; return, Sicilian Muſe,

And call the vales, and bid them hither caſt

Their bells, and flowrets of a thouſand hues.

Ye valleys low, where the mild whiſpers uſe

Of ſhades, and wanton winds, and guſhing brooks,

On whoſe freſh lap the ſwart ſtar ſparely looks,

Throw hither all your quaint enamel'd eyes,

That on the green turf ſuck the honied ſhowers,

And purple all the ground with vernal flowers:

Bring the rathe primroſe that forſaken dies,

The tufted crow-toe, and pale jeſſamine,

The white pink, and the panſy freakt with jet,

The glowing violet,

The muſk-roſe, and the well-attir'd woodbine,

With cowſlips wan that hang the penſive head,

And every flower that ſad embroidery wears:

Bid Amaranthus all his beauty ſhed,

And daffadillies fill their cups with tears,

To

To ftrew the laureat hearfe where LYCID lies:

For fo to interpofe a little eafe,

Let our frail thoughts dally with falfe furmife.

Ay me! Whilft thee the fhores, and founding feas

Wafh far away; where'er thy bones are hurl'd,

Whether beyond the ftormy Hebrides,

Where thou perhaps under the whelming tide

Vifit'ft the bottom of the monftrous world;

Or whether thou, to our moift vows deny'd,

Sleep'ft by the fable of Bellerus old,

Where the great vifion of the guarded mount

Looks toward Namancos and Bayona's hold;

Look homeward Angel now, and melt with ruth:

And, O ye dolphins, waft the haplefs youth.

Weep no more, woeful fhepherds, weep no more,

For LYCIDAS your forrow is not dead,

Sunk though he be beneath the watery floor;

So finks the day-ftar in the ocean bed,

And yet anon repairs his drooping head,

And tricks his beams, and with new-fpangled ore

Flames

Flames in the forehead of the morning ſky:

So LYCIDAS ſunk low, but mounted high,

Through the dear might of him that walk'd the waves,

Where other groves and other ſtreams along,

With nectar pure his oozy locks he laves,

And hears the unexpreſſive nuptial ſong,

In the bleſt kingdoms meek of joy and love;

There entertain him all the Saints above,

In ſolemn troops, and ſweet ſocieties,

That ſing, and ſinging in their glory move,

And wipe the tears for ever from his eyes.

Now, LYCIDAS, the ſhepherds weep no more;

Henceforth thou art the genius of the ſhore,

In thy large recompence, and ſhalt be good

To all that wander in that perilous flood.

    Thus ſang the uncouth ſwain to the oaks and rills;

While the ſtill morn went out with ſandals gray,

He touch'd the tender ſtops of various quills,

With eager thought warbling his Doric lay:

And

And now the fun had ftretch'd out all the hills,

And now was dropt into the weftern bay ;

At laft he rofe, and twitch'd his mantle blue :

To-morrow to frefh woods, and paftures new.

THE END.

CONTENTS.